Literary AllShorts
Volume 2

Short Stories from the
Ten Green Jotters

Published by TGJ
www.tengreenjotters.com

For all those who seize the day

'Never put off till tomorrow what you can read today' – *Holbrook Jackson*

PREFACE

Welcome to the fourth anthology of short stories by the Ten Green Jotters.

Literary AllShorts Volume 2 is a mix of adventure, romance, humour and horror written for the reader who wishes to escape the everyday humdrum of life!

We hope that you enjoy these 23 eclectic and thought-provoking tales plus 7 poems.

Ten Green Jotters 2024

CONTENTS

SAMAN AND ROMAN
By Houria Gheran

Once, nestling in the rugged mountains of Afghanistan, there lay a tiny village. A place where ancient traditions held strong, and the people lived a very simple life, following the religious path and some of the strict traditions of Afghanistan. It was in this village that two children were born on the same fateful day, though to different families—Saman, a spirited girl with fire in her eyes, and Roman, a kind-hearted boy with dreams as vast as the sky. Their families were close, bound by ties of friendship and mutual respect.

As the children grew, Saman and Roman became inseparable, sharing every joy, every sorrow, and every secret. They also shared an unbreakable bond with each other. They were known in the village as the "twin flames," their bond so strong that many believed they were destined for a shared future. But what no one knew, not even Saman and Roman, was that a bond far deeper, far more binding, had been forged between them since the very day they were born.

In a small village such as this, it was not uncommon for nursing mothers to share their milk with other babies in need. Out of necessity and compassion, as well as strict adherence to ancient Afghan traditions, Saman's mother had nursed Roman alongside her own daughter during a difficult time, creating a bond that, according to Afghan tradition, was as sacred as blood. Saman and Roman had become "milk siblings," a connection that made them family in the eyes of the law and the village. However, this fact remained a secret, locked away in the hearts of the two mothers who had nursed them. They had never imagined that these two people would develop feelings for each other that went beyond mere friendship and a sibling bond.

1

As Saman and Roman grew older, their friendship blossomed into something deeper, something more profound. Childhood games gave way to stolen glances and whispered words of love and the desire to be married and finally live together as husband and wife. They dreamt of a life together, a future where they could escape the confines of their small village and build a new world, side by side. They loved each other with a passion and never wanted to be separated. Moreover, their families got along well, and everyone was always happy to see them together. It was a given that both families would be delighted if, and when, Roman and Saman were joined in marriage.

But just as their love reached its peak, the truth was revealed. On a cold, windswept evening, as the village elders gathered to discuss the potential marriage, the mothers of Saman and Roman came forward with the truth that shattered their world.

"You cannot marry," Saman's mother said, her voice trembling with the weight of the confession. "You are milk siblings."

The words hung in the air like a death sentence. The ancient tradition, upheld by the village and enshrined in Afghan culture, dictated that milk siblings were as close as brother and sister. Marriage between them was forbidden, a sin against both Islam—the religion they both followed—and their country.

Saman and Roman stood frozen, their dreams collapsing around them, their hearts breaking as their world changed immensely with that one sentence, as if their mothers had signed their death certificate with that one life-altering revelation. They had heard of this tradition before, but it had never seemed real, never something that could touch them. But now, it was their reality—a cruel twist of fate that neither could have imagined.

Saman's heart was a storm of confusion and rage. How could something so pure, so beautiful, be deemed wrong? How could an act of kindness, an ancient practice meant to save lives, now destroy theirs? To her, Roman was not a brother. He was her love, her future, her everything. The thought of losing him, of living a life without him, was unbearable.

Roman, too, was crushed. He could see the pain in Saman's eyes, and it mirrored his own. The life they had dreamt of was slipping away, taken by a tradition that felt senseless and unjust. Yet, in the eyes of their community, there was no escape, no way to defy a rule so deeply embedded in their culture.

Days passed, but the despair only deepened. The village buzzed with gossip and speculation, but neither Saman nor Roman could bear to face their families or each other. The love that had once filled them with joy now felt like a curse, a burden too heavy to carry.

One evening, as the sun dipped below the mountains and darkness crept over the village, Saman and Roman met in secret at its edge. They held each other tightly, knowing that this might be the last time they could share a moment like this. Their hearts ached with the injustice of it all, the unfairness of a world that would not allow them to be together.

"Roman," Saman whispered, her voice choked with tears, "I cannot live in a world where I cannot be with you."

Roman cupped her face in his hands, his own tears mingling with hers. "Nor can I, Saman. If we cannot be together here, then let us find a place where we can."

So, hand in hand, they made their way to the highest mountain overlooking their village, the place where they had spent so many days dreaming of their future. The moonlight bathed the landscape in a silver glow. If they couldn't be together on this earth, they would make sure they were together in heaven.

They stood at the edge, looking out at the world they were leaving behind, and with one final embrace, they closed their eyes and stepped forward into the void, their souls entwined as they fell, together, into the abyss.

The village awoke the next morning to the tragic news. The loss of Saman and Roman sent shockwaves through the community, a stark reminder of the power of tradition and the cost of love denied. The families were devastated, knowing that one ancient, senseless Afghan tradition had taken their loved ones away forever. Both families mourned not only the loss of their children but also the cruel fate that had kept them apart.

In the years that followed, the unique love story of Saman and Roman became legendary, a tragic tale passed down through generations. Some saw it as a warning, a testament to the unbreakable bonds of tradition. Others, however, whispered that it was a call for change, a plea from two young lovers whose only crime had been to defy a law that made no sense to their hearts.

But no matter how the story was told, one thing remained certain: Saman and Roman had found the peace they sought, free from the chains that had bound them in life. And perhaps, somewhere beyond the reach of ancient laws and earthly customs, they had found the happiness they had always longed for—together, forever, in a place where love knew no bounds.

Author's note:
To this day the ancient act of milk sharing and becoming "milk siblings" still exists in Afghanistan.

MIRROR, MIRROR
By C.G. Harris

O wad some Pow'r the giftie gie us
To see oursels as ithers see us!

Robert Burns

Aye, Burns' words from *'To a Louse'* I recall with ease, for at noon upon one sultry day when brief blows through an open window brought no respite to my leaking brow, a visitor I received.

My office, one floor up and accessible by stairs that were wooden, hand-railed and worn, found deposited within it a curious being, or so it seemed to me at that moment.

The knock had been firm enough, and when I bade him enter there stood before me a man so disfigured and crooked that it took all my lawyerly self-control not to recoil; yet recognising my discomfiture still he smiled warmly to put me at my ease, and I motioned to the hard-backed chair across the desk at which I sat. The brief silence was broken only by the desultory clatter of hooves as cabs made their way down Princes Street.

"You have a reputation, sir, as a solicitor of honourable standing," he said, sitting with difficulty in his misshapen form; his voice was gentle, but not timid. He placed his cane upon the desk; upon removing his sleek top hat, I was able to fully regard his face. It was such a face as to inspire both fear and compassion, though as I was to learn there had been little of the latter in his life.

He had a visage lopsided and squat, his jaw was uneven and protruding and his upper lip was pulled to one side so that one canine was permanently on show, whether he smiled or no. His eyes were set in dark hollows, although this latter was no doubt due to a lifetime of strain and illness – his skin looked pale and wan – but the eyes themselves…ah! One was drawn to them – intelligent and bright, there was humour and warmth within.

"I thank you, sir," I replied. "Mr…?"

"Crosby. Or at least it is the name I was assigned."

"I see," I said, though in truth I did not. "What can I -"

He raised one crooked finger.

"If I may… I will soon come to purposes."

I nodded as he began his story; that of triumph over adversity, I discovered, at least to a degree.

"I knew not my mother or my father, because they did not wish to know me." He indicated himself with a wave of his hand. "Can you blame them? I do not. The orphanage at which I was left were kind in their way…although the other children not so. Cruelty begins at a young age."

For the first time his face clouded, although briefly. Then he smiled, and I know not why but it lifted me from within.

"Prospects were not auspicious, eh sir? Yet there are still some in the world with compassion. Watson's Poor School was the saving of me. Education, sir. Oh, there were beatings from some masters, kindness from others – that is one kind of education. The attainment of knowledge is the other; I learned. I learned, so that when I left, it behove me to become a man of means. At each point along the way, rabid taunts and stares accompanied me and no companion had I for long, lonely years. I resigned myself to a life alone…until Jacqueline."

He paused and closed his eyes to recollect the better.

"A beauty, a rare, kind beauty from the Kirk, who seemed not to see what others saw. Oh, I know that compassion was at first the draw, but sir!" He placed both hands upon the desk. "I know also," he whispered, "that her compassion turned to love."

I was silent, for I feared what he was to say next.

6

"Aye," he said, softly. "A mutual love, a proposal, acceptance... it was too much to believe that such happiness would be finally mine! And so, it was. I stood before the altar that day – with few enough to see, thank God! And waited. She was late, I told myself... then later still. She was so very late, but I waited further whilst my heart moved and sank and broke within me until I found myself alone in silence with just holy stone walls to see my grief... She did not appear, you see."

He stood with difficulty and shallow breath.

"As with my mother... I do not blame. It was much to ask of her. She married another."

I was quiet for a moment. "And now...?"

"And now, sir, I have but a month to live. She has a husband no more, but a boy. A fine, healthy boy. I have seen them from afar – I wish that he were mine, but he is not, yet still I rejoice for them. But circumstances are not good, and straights are dire; hardship and penury beckon for them, if nothing is done."

He picked up his cane and hat and drew himself up as straight as he could.

"Write this down, sir, if you will! One thousand guineas straight away to the Watsons School. And when I finally rest, my fortune to the lady and the boy."

With faltering step, he turned to go, but I stopped him and clasped his hand.

"You have done well, sir," I said, softly.

He nodded, and the eyes sparkled.

I cannot say what others see, but I saw the most noble and beautiful man I had ever met.

BRIEFS ENCOUNTER
By Tony Ormerod

'Fancy seeing you!'

The young man approached me, smiled as he spoke and then laughed out loud. Pretending for a moment or two that I did not recognise him did not work; he was not fooled. Spotting the lad with a gang of youths at the far end of the bar a minute or so before, I had fervently hoped that he had not remembered me. After all, I was some distance from my normal stamping ground and I had deliberately dressed down. Curiosity had led me to that public house.

'Do you come here often?' He was smirking now.

'Er, no. As a matter of fact, I was passing by and I felt thirsty so I...'

'Just popped in for a quick one?' he suggested, enjoying my obvious discomfort.

'Yes, that's it of course; nice beer here.' I drained my half pint glass and looked anxiously towards the exit.

'You're not going now surely? Let me buy you another please' He reached into his back pocket and withdrew a bundle of notes.

'No thank you, er, John, is it? One is plenty for me; thank you again but I must be going' I looked frantically at my watch. 'Goodness is that the time?'

'Actually, it's Jim'

'What is? Oh sorry, yes of course, your name. Silly me!'

'Can't expect you to remember all of us.' Patting me on my arm in a condescending manner, which annoyed me intensely, he added, 'After all I only turn up on high days and holidays.'

Nodding in agreement then turning to go, desperate to get out as quickly as possible. I was too late. Two large speakers, either end of a small stage sprang noisily into life.

'The minute you walked in the joint I could tell you were a man of distinction, a real big spender.' That raucous Shirley Bassey number created quite a stir. The large crowd, some seated but the majority, standing, started cheering. Failing to see him emerging from the Gents toilet I collided violently with the scantily clad opening act who, together with an enormous snake, was about to leap onto the stage and into action. All three of us crashed into a table and then onto the floor, scattering pints and customers as we did so. Disaster!

For a couple of seconds, aside from Shirley, all was quiet. Then, some men laughed. Others booed as I extricated myself out of, and then up from the wreckage.

'You bloody fool, you bloody idiot!' yelled the artiste who was, by the way, billed as *'Victor and his Boa Constrictor.'* His matching bra and panties, originally a fetching shade of pink, were now liberally drenched with what I presumed was lager and Guinness.

'Can't you look where you're going?' he inquired angrily, but reasonably.

'Sorry. I...I...' Embarrassed, ashamed, damp and determined to escape I fled the scene. Just as I reached the door to the blessed sanctuary of the pavement a raised voice rang out above the din. Of course it was Jim's.

'Might see you in church sometime Vicar?'

EDEN
By Glynne Covell

Wild, romantic western land,
Perfection moulded by God's own hand.
Inviting coastal path lures walkers to tread
The way stretched out before,
Absorb, renew, and self-assure,
Life's meaning to implore.

Seagulls swooping, diving with shrieking whine,
Cry out, 'This land is mine!'
Rugged clifftops, slipping inclines,
Secluded caves and beaches,
Endless coastline, skyline, reaches.

Waves of sea thrift pink, gorse of yellow and bells of blue
Hugging twisting pathways, bedecked with every hue.
Aroma of pure air, fresh garlic, brine
On breezes cool, sou'west entwine.

Patient surfers on boards await
One rides high; others try, one too late.
The sea it roars, crashes, creeps;
Sucking sand from shelving land
As if drawing breath by lunar hand.

Inwards, outwards, hour by hour
Soothing, thrilling show of power
Clear night skies of shooting stars and Milky Way
Glorious sunrise heralds another day.

Comfort pasties, scones and cream,
Chips from paper, mackerel, bream.

Harbour jumping at high tide
Choughs a-searching high and wide.

Cornwall is my Eden, Cornwall is in my heart
This land is my tonic, my compass, and my chart.

A VISIT TO THE DENTIST
By Julia Gale

I woke one morning after a restless night's sleep with a hell of a toothache that only worsened during the day. I'm not the greatest fan of the dentist, but after a bit of not-so-gentle persuasion from my wife, Helen, I finally decided it was now time to try and find one; not easy with the current state of the NHS and to boot we had recently moved into a new area. I had to accept that the pain wasn't going to go away by itself.

'Why don't you go on the computer and search for a local dentist who will accept new NHS patients?' Helen suggested craftily, knowing full well that if there is one thing I detest more than seeing the dentist it's going on the internet.

'Can't you do it?' I whined. 'You are better than me when it comes to computers.' I wasn't hopeful that she would; she told me to get on with it.

Protesting, but under my breath, I sat down and began my search. A couple of hours of this seemed like an eternity and after I had rung all the local surgeries with no joy, that was it, I gave up. Naturally, this did nothing to help my mood; the toothache was worsening and my backside was numb.

Calling for Helen and getting no answer, I recalled she'd told me she was going out to do something, I couldn't remember exactly what. I looked out of the window; she had taken the car.

'I'd be better off grabbing some rusty pliers from the shed and pulling it out myself,' I grumbled. I was tempted; I almost smiled, imagining Helen's reaction to the mess on her return.

I didn't do that, of course, but instead took another couple of paracetamols and grabbed from the freezer some whiskey ice cubes I'd made earlier. Popping them into my mouth, I sat down in the lounge to watch some afternoon TV.

I suppose I must have fallen asleep because the next thing I heard was the sound of something being pushed through the letterbox.

Wandering into the porch, I saw on the floor a leaflet from a local dentist. It was odd because this one hadn't appeared at all in the searches I'd made. There was a bold statement printed in red claiming to have the future of the profession in his hands. Normally I would have put something like this in the bin, but the timing was just right, it was a little bit different and it promised reassuringly that it was the practice of the future.

Buoyed up by this, I dragged my bike out from the garage to try and find the address on the leaflet; unusually, there was no telephone number I could ring in advance.

It took me a while but I found it somewhat off the beaten track, down streets well away from the main drag. When I finally arrived at a building it was not at all what I expected; it was old and decrepit and tucked away down a dingy alleyway.

First impressions inside were also not good. The waiting area was completely bare: no posters advertising products, no glossy magazines on a corner table, not even a fish tank. The receptionist, a stony-faced, expressionless woman, pushed a form at me and told me to sit down.

'Hardly the practice of the future,' I thought.

Out of the corner of my eye, I noticed a young woman dressed in a nurse's uniform, who appeared to be asleep on a chair in the corner.

13

'Quiet day today, is it?' I asked the receptionist. She didn't reply, just stared at me. I sat down in a hard chair and filled out the form.

My wait wasn't a long one and the receptionist suddenly rose and ushered me into a room. It was completely dark when I entered but, with a flash of light, a projection of a man appeared before me, dressed in a dental gown and wearing gloves.

'Hang on… what the … you're a hologram,' I stuttered.

'Yes, of course!' he replied. 'What did you expect? Now, lie on the couch Mr. -' he glanced at the form '- Brown, and open your mouth wide.'

My legs gave way; I somehow landed on the couch, exactly where he wanted me to be. He took the briefest of looks inside my mouth.

'What seems to be the problem?' he said.

I explained about my toothache, which had all but disappeared. There are worse things than toothache.

'Yeh. The whole lot will have to be removed,' he said, indifferently. He summoned his nurse, the same young lady I'd seen in the waiting room.

'This is Jenny, my assistant. She is specially programmed to extract teeth. AI, of course.' I looked around to see Jenny with a big smile on her manufactured face… She was holding a rusty set of pliers.

'You're not using those on me!' I whispered. 'I've… I've got my own at home, thanks.'

'Please don't worry – it won't hurt, you'll be fast asleep,' Jenny promised, reassuringly, producing a huge needle. I felt a sharp jab in my arm as the needle went right through my sleeve.

The room span; I was falling down a deep, dark hole. The hologram, Jenny and the receptionist followed. They were demanding loudly that I pay the million pounds I owed for the treatment. I couldn't stop myself from screaming, I really couldn't. It wasn't about the money... although I couldn't help thinking it was supposed to be NHS.

I landed with a bump.

I found myself lying on the living room floor, Helen looking at me with an unusually concerned expression on her face.

'I really believe it's time I took you to the hospital, don't you think?' she said. 'Although I did pick this up on my travels this afternoon; they look very good.'

She handed me a leaflet. It proclaimed, in bold red letters, that it was the dental practice of the future.

'God, no!' I shouted. 'Just take me to the hospital – please!'

ARTY FARTY
By Richie Stress

Arty Farty had a party
All the Farts were there
Tooty Fruity done a beauty
And they all went out for air.

Tummy Rumble began to grumble
And only stayed 'til four
Squeaky Sneaker grabbed a beaker
Then moonwalked out the door.

Barry Burp was such a twerp
He burped and burped all day
He belched so much that he lost touch
With no-one else to play.

Dozy Kelly found the telly
But there was nothing on
She fell asleep - when she woke
Everyone had gone.

Toby Jug broke his mug
Tho it was not malicious
He cleaned it up then had some cake
And said it was delicious.

Tappy Toes could strike a pose
If no-one else was looking
Then danced into the kitchen
To see what else was cooking.

Sally sneeze caused such a breeze
She sent the others flying
And if that wasn't bad enough
Cry Baby started crying.

So, Brenda Bell began to yell
And everyone fell silent
Arty shouted, 'Party's Over!'
'Please can you be quiet.'

So, this is how the guests all leave
The Arty Farty Fable
All except for Naughty Nik
Who hid under the table.

MY LEFT SHOE
By Jan Brown

I woke up with a banging headache and a mouth like a sewer, with an added appetiser that tasted of dirty cat fur. From what I could remember, though, it had been worth it: a fantastic night where I'd met the woman of my dreams. So, I should feel good, right? Well, yes, but I'd woken up in a field surrounded by a pack of cows: curious cows staring down at me, masticating slowly and thoughtfully. I scrambled to my feet. *Grow up, Martin. Cows can't think.*

As I moved, they began to move with me, and I admit I panicked. I'd read about people getting crushed by cows, particularly those who fell asleep in their field, so I began to run, or jog really, I wasn't a runner.

"Ouch!"

The pain was unbearable as I crunched down on a rock or stone in my haste to get away. I looked down at my foot, which was already turning red, and then looked again. I only had one shoe. My right foot was still encased in its black *Nike Air Revolution* trainer, but my left foot was not. It stood naked and defenceless, and red, and sore. The cow pack had easily kept up with me and as, I stood uncertainly looking around (for I realised I had no idea where I was), I shuddered as a huge raspy pink tongue curled itself around my naked left foot and licked enthusiastically.

My phone! I pulled my Nokia500 out of my back pocket, praying there was some battery. Yes, battery was fine, but no signal. I stomped around the rocky, muddy field thrusting my phone in the air like Doctor ruddy Who waving his sonic screwdriver, but I couldn't get a signal. The cows followed me on my field journey, not in a threatening way, but curious. If they could talk, they would probably be asking what the hell I was doing.

"Moo," said a cow.

"Where's my bloody trainer?" I asked it.

I hobbled on, trying to keep my left foot safe from the sharp stones hidden in the grass and mud, and became aware of a loud snort from one of the cows who seemed much more thick-set than her friends. She had a hump back, poor girl, and appeared quite angry at the world, digging and pawing at the ground.

"Get away from the bull!" somebody screamed at me. "This way! Quickly now... No, don't run – and don't turn your back on him. Just keep moving, damn you."

All these instructions appeared completely contradictory to me: *get away, move, don't run, keep moving.* If I made it out alive, I would tell him so.

I moved slowly backwards, the bull in my periphery vision and my heart thumping so loudly the whole bovine gang must have heard it. I didn't know whether to look at it or not; which would he consider to be a lesser challenge to his undoubted masculine superiority?

"Get in." The farmer – I presumed him to be so – slowed his jeep sufficiently to allow me to throw myself into the passenger seat and sped off as the bull began to gather speed. "Shut the bloody door, man," he instructed, before immediately asking, "What were you doing in my field? Trying to steal my cattle, were you?"

"No, no, of course not. I woke up in your field. I don't even know how I got there, and I've lost my shoe. I couldn't get a signal to phone anyone, and I met the most amazing woman last night and I can't even remember her name."

"Hmm, women. More trouble than they are value." He said no more, but sucked noisily on his dentures, shifting them in and out with the ease of an IKEA salesperson opening and closing built-in drawers.

"Why have you only got one shoe?" he said, eventually. "Is it one of those initiation ceremonies? Something to do with losing your virginity, no doubt?"

"I told you, I lost my shoe, and I'm lost. There is no initiation ceremony, and I lost my virginity when I was 14 with Karen Dymond." My saviour was making me uneasy. That was the only explanation I could think of for giving out my deepest secrets, and my vocabulary was shot... three *'losts'* in one sentence.

"Hmm, if you say so. Bit too much protesting if you ask me, young man. Why would I need to know the name of your first victim?"

"What? What... what are you on about? What victim?"

He cackled. "You're definitely a townie! No sense of humour. Any road, it's the end of the line for you, sonny boy."

"What do you mean?" I squeaked, trying to control the contortions in my stomach.

He brought the jeep to a standstill and gestured to the crossroad signs. "I mean, I'm going home that way – and you're not." He looked at me pointedly and, when I made no effort to move, leaned across me and opened the door. "Out."

"But I don't know where I am."

"Well, it's about time you grew up and found out, isn't it? I've no time for cattle thieves. Now, out of my jeep." The stubble on his chin bristled angrily as he glared at me.

"I'm not a thief!"

I was shouting at him now, but he had some strength as he pushed me out onto the road and slammed the vehicle into first gear. I stood on the road staring after him until the dust had settled, and the general silence was broken by gentle twittering from the trees.

My foot was still throbbing, but I tried to walk or hobble, keeping an ear open for any approaching traffic. I took my phone out again and stared at it hopefully. Yes! There was a signal. I flicked through the contents; undecided who to call, I scrolled the names up and down. "Choose someone, you idiot," I muttered. Finally settling on a number, I dialled.

"Hello, Marjory Barnes speaking. Who is this please?"

"Mum, it's me. Martin."

"Why Mart'n, how lovely to hear from my best boy. How are you?"

I tried to jump in while she took a breath. "I'm OK, Mum, but I had a bit of a mishap last night and I'm a bit lost."

"Oh my God, whatever have you been up to now, Mart'n? I knew nothing good would come of you going to that college. Did I not say that very thing to your Uncle Nobby only the other day? Will you listen to me now about coming back home? You're a kind boy but you have a weak will. Easily led, like your poor father."

"Mum!" I shouted. "I've only got one shoe."

"What in God's name are you up to running around with one shoe? Although if your feet are anything like your father's, I'd be surprised if you're moving at all. Your father's side of the family were never the ones for having good solid feet."

The abrupt silence on my mobile wasn't good and my worst fears were confirmed. The battery was totally flat. Even if I were standing next to Nokia HQ, I'd get nothing out of my phone now. I limped on, past endless fields and hedgerows, occasionally leaping into said hedge as cars sped by, too near for comfort.

Grey clouds were rushing in now, angry and swirling, bringing with them a gusty, enthusiastic wind. Huge splotches of rain began drumming down and splashing onto the road, churning up the already unsettled earth. My dirty left foot was soaked and numb.

21

A sudden movement through the rain-soaked trees caught my eye and I stared desperately. Was it the farmer? Probably not. What would he be doing, lurking about? "Damn that man," I muttered. "Why couldn't the fool have just given me a lift back to civilisation? If I ever see him again, I'll give him what for."

I stewed and moaned about my unfortunate situation and eventually found some salvation from the rain by sheltering under a large tree with strong, generous branches and full foliage. Thankfully, there was no sign of thunder or lightning. Finally, after what felt like an eternity, the rain slowed to a spatter and a weak sun emerged, glinting and glittering on swollen leaves. A few birds in the branches began to whistle optimistically and I actually heard the splodge as it was released from above and landed directly on the shoulder of my jacket.

"Nooo!" I screamed. "What have I done to deserve all this? Why? Why? I'm never going to get out of here."

The birds were silenced and, with a grimace at my stained jacket, I left my dubious shelter and continued hobbling down the road, angry and preoccupied with my bad luck. I wasn't prepared for the car that came hurtling along the road behind me until almost at the last second. I threw myself again into the hedge.

"You bloody idiot!" I tried to shout, but that's always difficult when you have your face in a hedge.

The approaching footsteps tapped daintily. "I'm so sorry. Are you OK?" Her voice was concerned and cultured. She leaned over me and I got subtle hints of perfume; goodness knows what, but it was nice. "Here, let me help you." She helped me to my feet and began brushing me down, curling her lip as she avoided the obvious stain that had settled in nicely against the green of my jacket.

She looked around her in confusion "You seem to have lost a shoe. Again, I'm so sorry. It must have travelled quite a way."

I couldn't help grinning at her like a fool, probably on the edge of hysteria. "You could say that."

"Well, you'll probably need a new pair anyway by the time you find it. Come on, let's get you back to civilisation."

I relaxed into the comfortable fabric of the front seat. Lulled by the gentle purring of the engine, I found my eyes shutting and my head nodding forward.

Suddenly, she said: "Oops. I need to stop for these gentlemen. It's OK, I'm not in the habit of picking up random men – although I have literally just picked you up off the ground." She smiled at my guarded expression. "Don't worry, I know them from croquet."

As the car slowed to a halt, the two guys were already jogging over. "Cindy, what a stroke of luck." The taller of the two grinned and nodded at me and I couldn't help noticing the gaps in his mouth where teeth should have been. His shorter companion (did he have a neck in that collar?) just grunted in my direction.

"I know, isn't it, darlings? I seem to be collecting men lately. Better late than never, I suppose." She giggled.

"What's your name then, mate?" Both had got into the back of the car, and the tall man now leaned forward and breathed the fumes of a thousand beers down at me.

"Martin," I squeaked weirdly, as it's difficult to speak and hold your breath at the same time.

"Pleased to meet ya. I'm Steve the Sleeve. You struck lucky with Cindy 'ere."

"Right, yes. You have an interesting name."

Cindy giggled again, now less cultured, and more breathless teenager. "Yes, bless both these boys. They've certainly added a little something extra to the croquet club."

Free dentistry – or neck extensions? I wondered to myself, silently of course.

"Steve's always got a little deal going on, always got something up his sleeve," she trilled.

They all laughed uproariously and Steve the Sleeve grabbed me – affectionately, I think, although it was difficult to see the expression on his face crushed as I was in the folds of his jacket. I struggled up for air and sucked in large draughts of beer fumes.

"What about your friend?" I asked.

"What about me?" The other back seat passenger responded aggressively.

"Errr…" I stuttered. "I just wondered what your name is."

"Why? What do you want to know for?" As he leant forward over the front seat and close to my face, I could see his eyes were a sort of bloodshot grey, tiny veins running through like cracks in a dried-out pavement.

"Just making conversation. I mean, I don't have to know your name, it's not a problem if I don't know your name, it's fine." I babbled on, suddenly aware they were surveying me like benevolent uncles.

"He's No Neck Nick," Steve the Sleeve shouted joyously as I jumped in shock. "And do you know why?"

I shook my head as they all continued shouting in unison. "He's got no neck, his name's No Neck Nick."

I shrank into the seat as the shouting and laughter raged on until finally Cindy pulled the car up outside a low concrete building signposted 'Durley Social Club.'

"OK. my darlings, it's been lovely to catch up. You must all come round for a little snifter one evening – and bring Tiffany, Flopsy and Barnaby, of course."

Children or rabbits? I wondered, all the while thinking, *yes, he has no neck.*

"Mate." Steve the Sleeve advanced on me. "It's been a pleasure to meet another of Cindy's friends." He breathed 100% pure alcohol into my face and winked in an exaggerated manner that, weirdly, caused his left eye to close and his mouth to open simultaneously, revealing the toothless cavern within. He marched off towards the entrance, followed by No Neck Nick who, lacking a neck, simply moved his entire head up and down. He stood at the entrance and stared at us both, I think longingly at Cindy and suspiciously at me, before following his taller companion inside.

"Well, I assume you weren't looking for Durley Social Club. Is there a plan for your day?" Cultured Cindy had reappeared.

"I'm looking for a girl I met last night, and then I got lost."

She twitched her small, perfect nose. "Does she have your missing shoe? Was it a theft? Is that why you're looking for her?"

"No, no, I lost that while I was in the field. I have no idea where it is but that's not important. It's her – she's wonderful. I think I'm in love with her and I need to find her. I can't even remember her name."

"Hmm, quite. You do seem very careless. Lost people, shoes, names, and yourself." She turned on the engine and stared at me. "So careless. You'd better come to the farmhouse and you can call a responsible adult – if you know one, of course. Goodness knows what Max will think of me picking up another stray."

We sat in silence as the car hurtled along deserted country lanes, my teeth clenched rigidly every time we shot round a blind corner, until finally we drove between impressive stone pillars and came to a halt outside a large building that I considered to be more medium-sized hotel than house.

"No key? I see I'm not the only one for losing things," I said, trying for a joke as she slammed down the huge lion head door knocker three times.

A man in a black suit almost immediately answered the door and I looked around desperately for a hole to hide in. She apparently didn't need to carry a key.

"Mrs. Carmichael. Welcome home." I swear he bowed.

"Thank you, Jenkins. This young man has managed to get lost. He needs to telephone someone, preferably someone intelligent. Is Max around?"

"He's in the drawing room, madam, with Isabella."

She sashayed off in the indicated direction, and the name hit me as I remembered; I shouted with delight. "That's it. Isabella! That's her name. Isabella."

The heavy wooden door opened and I stared at a familiar face, lit from behind by a sparkling chandelier. "What the hell are you doing here?" the farmer growled. "Still looking for cattle to steal?"

"Oh Daddy, don't be so mean to him now." I could see Isabella behind him, laughing. "He's harmless, and he's probably looking for that." She waved at my lost shoe, clutched in her father's paw.

"Cindy, what's this ruffian doing in my house?" He glared at me. "I warned you; I don't like thieves."

"Enough!" I felt like I was disappearing down the rabbit hole from hell but found energy from somewhere to shout. "I've been looking for you all day, Isabella. I think I love you – and I'm not a thief! How many times do I have to say that, sir? And why have you got my shoe? What's going on?"

"Well, Max, you've been found out with your little test," Mrs. Carmichael, or Cindy, drawled. "What do you think? Has he passed? He coped very well with the boys earlier."

His eyes narrowed as he sucked again on his dentures; thoughtfully, I hoped. Either that or he had indigestion. He

26

advanced towards me, gesturing with my shoe. "First of all, you need to learn how to behave around my cattle and my daughter."

"What did your wife mean about your test?"

"Oh. come on, sonny boy. I've got to protect my assets. I'm not having some chancer waltz in."

The chandelier had suddenly lost its lustre "So all this was a set up?" I asked into the awkward silence.

"I'm sure I was worth a bit of effort." Isabella, still as gorgeous as I remembered, leant in for a kiss and I recoiled.

"You put me through all that, for what? Your weird father thinking I'm after the family treasures? I'm not that desperate."

On reflection, of course that hadn't been the best response. That reflection is coming easily to me as I'm lying in my hospital bed with a black eye and two broken ribs. I do have my shoe though, and there's a nurse on the night shift who is rather cute.

THE DARK SIDE OF THE SUN
By Richard Miller

To celebrate the end of their time at university, six students who had recently graduated decided to head to Dorset for a week. There was Richard, Jack, Stuart, Rosie, Kathy, and Diana. They weren't couples, just good friends who had shared a house while studying.

The train journey to Weymouth was uneventful: just the usual chatter, reading, listening to music, and the occasional alcoholic drink. On arrival, they checked into the hotel.

"Let's head into town, have a wander around, and plan for the next few days," suggested Jack, whose idea of planning usually involved visiting a pub.

"Two days of walking, a few days on the beach, and end with some more walking. How does that sound?" declared Rosie. She was always the one who organised everything and everyone.

After spending two days walking, the group headed to Lulworth Cove to relax on the beach. They wouldn't spend too much time sunbathing, given the recent government warnings about climate change and the dangers of skin cancer. Maybe a bit of swimming. Kathy and Richard were strong swimmers, while Stuart and Diana didn't mind a dip. Jack and Rosie, however, couldn't swim.

"Kathy, fancy a swim?" Richard asked. "What about you, Stuart, and Diana? The sea's calm. We can swim to Durdle Door and back—it shouldn't take too long."

"Yes," Kathy answered.

Diana and Stuart looked at the sea and the sky, both of which were clear, and said in unison, "Why not."

Jack glanced at Rosie and spoke on behalf of them both. "We'd love to join you, but we can't, for obvious reasons. We'll look after your stuff."

The four of them ran into the sea and began their swim to one of Dorset's most famous natural landmarks.

The plan, once they arrived at Durdle Door, was to sit on the rocks and rest for a while. However, when they were about two-thirds of the way there, Stuart and Diana decided to return to the beach as they were feeling cold.

"No worries," shouted Kathy. "Me and Richard will carry on and be back later. Don't drink all the wine!"

A few minutes later, the pair reached their destination. "Come on, Kathy. We can sit on these rocks," Richard suggested.

At that moment, the sky turned dark, and soon after, lightning and thunder began. They realised they'd have to stay put until the weather improved before swimming back. As they neared the beach, Kathy said, "Something's wrong. I can see people, but they look different. It doesn't feel right."

"Are you sure?" Richard replied, but as soon as he spoke, he sensed it too—something was different.

They crawled out of the water and headed towards their friends. As soon as they saw them, they knew something was wrong. The friends had aged about forty years.

Diana spoke first. "What the bloody hell! It can't be. You two are supposed to be dead. And why do you look so young? Is this some kind of sick joke?"

"Sorry," replied Kathy. "What do you mean, dead? You went swimming with us about two hours ago. You and Stuart headed back, but we were at Durdle Door waiting for the bad weather to clear. And you all look so old. We're all twenty-two or twenty-three, but you look about sixty."

Richard looked around at everyone else on the beach. No one looked young, not even the kids. All the people, including their friends, were covered from head to toe. You'd always see some people covering up due to sensitive skin, but this was different. They were aware of the government's warnings, but surely things couldn't have changed so drastically in just a few hours.

"We may look sixty, but we're only in our early thirties. That's what climate change and the sun's rays do to you now," Diana explained. "And when I said you were dead, I meant it. When you didn't come back, we called the coastguard and the lifeboat. They couldn't find you, and you were presumed dead. A funeral was held. Your parents were distraught. We've been coming here for fifteen years, on the anniversary of your deaths, to raise a glass to absent friends. Your parents came for a while, but your fathers have passed away, and your mothers moved away and cut all ties. And now you suddenly reappear from nowhere."

"Fifteen years?" It was Richard's turn to look stunned. "What do you mean, fifteen years? As Kathy said, we've only been gone a couple of hours."

"If you don't believe us," Rosie chimed in, "look at the newspaper."

She threw Richard the paper, and he gasped when he saw the date. He showed it to Kathy, who was just as shocked.

"I don't understand. Kathy and I are as baffled as you are. Kathy, any ideas?" Richard asked.

"None. Unless—no, that can't be right—something happened when we were at Durdle Door. Time travel?"

Stuart shouted, "Time travel? What a load of old tosh. You'd better not be playing a joke."

"Don't be silly," Kathy shot back. "Look at us. We look exactly the same as when we swam out to Durdle Door. Why would we do that, especially when Richard and I have jobs lined up? We left our phones, keys, and other stuff with Jack and Rosie since they didn't swim. Isn't that right, Rosie?"

"Yep," Rosie confirmed.

Jack, who had been quiet until now, finally spoke. "We're overlooking something, aren't we? Kathy and

Richard, you won't know what I'm talking about, but the rest of you will."

Diana, Rosie, and Stuart all nodded.

"What do you mean?" Richard asked.

"Because of the dramatic changes to the climate, it's now dangerous and illegal to be out in the sun's rays for too long without being covered up. You could be fined or even imprisoned. You two stand out like sore thumbs. Remember the rules about COVID and how people were fined? Well, it's like that. Look, Rosie and I have some clothes you can wear."

Just then, a voice came from a few yards away. "Why are you out and about without being covered up? You know the rules."

Richard turned to see three policemen. He heard Diana say, "They don't know the rules. They've been away for a while."

"What do you mean?" one of the officers asked. "The rules have been well-publicised for years. They were made for everyone's safety."

"Sir, we honestly don't know the rules," Richard said. "We were only away from the beach for a couple of hours, not fifteen years, as you and our friends believe."

"You can tell that to our boss at the local station—and then the magistrate."

"Diana, Rosie, Jack, Stuart—help us," Kathy pleaded. They moved to join them.

"Stay where you are with one of my colleagues," the policeman ordered. "We'll let you know when we need you. Right, come on, you two. Follow us." Kathy and Richard were taken to a police van. "Get in the back."

The journey to the police station took about twenty minutes. In that time, they were given some clothes to wear. On arriving at the station, they were taken to an interview room. A few minutes later, a plainclothes officer walked in.

31

"Right, my name is DI Tom Roberts. And you are?"

The pair gave their names.

"So, you know why you're here? Not being properly dressed," Roberts began.

"Sir," Kathy spoke up, "we honestly don't know the rules. For us, it's the year 2024. But I can see the calendar on the wall says 2039."

"Can you prove that?" asked Roberts.

"You'll have to ask our friends. We left all our stuff with them when we went for a swim," Richard said.

"We'll do that," Roberts replied. Turning to a constable, he added, "Constable, bring their friends here."

"Yes, sir."

"In the meantime, here are some straightforward questions for you, or they should be. Let's see how you get on with these. Who is the Prime Minister? Who won the FA Cup? Where will the next Olympics be held?"

"Rishi Sunak, Manchester United, and Los Angeles. I assume you mean the 2028 Summer Olympics," Richard answered.

Roberts raised an eyebrow. "Interesting. We'll wait for your friends."

Forty minutes later, the constable entered the room. "They're here, sir."

"Send the first one in. It doesn't matter who. Take these two to another room and then come back," Roberts instructed.

Diana entered the room.

"Please sit down. Name?"

"Diana Wilson."

"So, you know the two people who just left the room. When did you last see them?" Roberts asked.

"Fifteen years ago. They went swimming to Durdle Door. A storm blew up, and they disappeared. We called the coastguard and the lifeboat. Later, they were presumed dead. Then, today, they turn up, looking the same as when they disappeared, while we've aged, thanks to the bloody sun's rays," Diana explained.

"Do you believe them?"

"I don't know. At first, I thought they were pulling a fast one, but it would be some trick, that's for sure, and for no reason. And I have to say, even if they tried to fool us, they wouldn't upset their parents. That's not their way."

"What did you do with their stuff?"

"We gave everything to their parents. You won't track down the fathers—they're both dead. And the mothers cut ties and moved away. Can't say I blame them; it must have been heartbreaking. And no, Richard and Kathy didn't have siblings. I don't know about aunts or uncles."

Rosie, Stuart, and Jack were invited in and gave the same account as Diana.

"Constable, bring our two suspects in here and stay with them. I'll take the others to the canteen. Then I need to think about this," Roberts said.

He returned to his office, locked the door, unlocked a cabinet and pulled out a file. Normally, everything was stored on computers, but certain topics were so sensitive that only a few people in the UK—and the world—were privy to them. In addition to being an officer in Dorset Police, Roberts also worked for MI6. Only the Chief Constable of Dorset Police knew that. Roberts had been recruited by MI6 some time ago and was sworn to secrecy about his role in the organisation.

The file showed a list of people around the world who had disappeared and reappeared without ageing. This was the first time such an occurrence had been reported in the UK.

He pondered what to do but knew he had to call his boss at MI6 for a decision.

"Boss, we have a problem. Two people who disappeared have reappeared, and they haven't aged. Should I send them to you? Also, there are four witnesses who claim to be their friends."

"Yes, send all six to me. I'll send two vans down."

Three hours later, two vans arrived in Weymouth. After some time, they headed to London—one van with four passengers, the other with two.

Two days later, Roberts read an article about a van that had crashed. The driver and a guard had escaped. Four others in the van had been burnt beyond all recognition. As for the other van, Roberts knew that was for someone else in MI6 to worry about. He also knew that only a few people in the world would be aware of what happened to the reappeared.

I AM
By Glynne Covell

I am.

I am a house, a home, a dwelling, a shelter. I am proud to have stood so long and now that I am so very old, there are endless memories woven within my walls, tales of long ago, days of fear and trouble, sorrow together with happiness, fun and laughter.

I came into being in the third quarter of the year 1599. It took nearly that whole year of painstaking labour, men working through all weathers before I was complete. An exciting and awesome year as I gradually grew and took shape in the road that led to the castle. The first of many abodes that joined me in the shadow of Corfe. My crowning glory was my thatched roof.

How very splendid I looked that day in Spring when the family of Zachariah moved in, the young children happy and excited to explore every nook and cranny while the good doctor set up his practice in the corner of the main room. His wife tended to the garden, planting her numerous medicinal herbs for potions, lotions, and tinctures to support her husband's work. Happy days. I stood proudly protective of my inhabitants, sheltering them from the forces of nature as, year by year, the children grew.

Dark, dark, stormy days were to follow. Gruesome times. Days upon which I hardly dare to dwell, save to say that I have never seen the like again through the centuries.

It was the civil war, during the reign of Charles I and the Roundheads, with their distinctive short haircuts, who attacked the castle walls relentlessly; murdering, hacking their way through until those within the stronghold yielded to the slaughtering. I shuddered and trembled with the noise of the horrendous cannon fire mixed with the blood-curdling screams of the injured and dying. The road before me was red with blood and bodies.

Zachariah was quite old by this time but still he helped as much as he could; with so many others, the dying end their days quickly when there was no hope to save them. It took many weeks to bury the dead and adjust to a near normal life. The smell of rotting corpses lasted for so long and my timbers seemed to absorb the nauseous stench. Enough! Enough!

So, through the centuries, I have seen good and bad times. The coming and going of families who I grew to love as I sheltered them from inclement weather, cocooning them with the security of my thick walls. I have listened passively to the trials and tribulations of family life. I have witnessed in awe many inventions and improvements for easier living than when I first came about. Running water, electricity, drainage and, these days, the incredible technology that seems to control human life. I do not begin to understand, and do not want to understand this powerful force. But the basic needs of those souls who I continue to shelter are the same: love, health, and happiness.

I have had my problems, which, sadly, seem to increase with age! My foundations are too shallow and there has been considerable leaning of my rear walls. They have now been shored up with supports. My windows have been changed and restored with new modern frames and are less draughty than before. I creak and groan with age when the wind gets high and whistles through my cracks.

It was a frightening time when I was first rethatched. I was sad and felt bereft when they stripped me of the old straw; I thought I had come to the end of my days. The mice and insects who made their home in my crowning glory scampered away if they could, as I lay bare. But oh, the joy and pleasure when master thatchers arrived and set about restoring my roof. It looks remarkably easy, but I can tell you, it is a skilful art to use and trim the straw, reeds, and rushes to produce such a brilliant, creative thatch, adorned with the impression of two peacocks. The wildlife soon returned to inhabit my cosy roof.

I suffer from woodworm in my timbers, so need to be continuously monitored. But hey, I am old: in my senior years. The aged need care.

Ah, I have had a good life. Here and now, in the autumn of my days, I stand quietly and thoughtfully in the road that leads to Corfe Castle. These days I witness many more invasions but this time, they are friendly. So many more people are seen in this village and, quite often, the crowds amaze me. The castle itself is now a ruin - but a beautiful ruin. Many people flock to see it, paying for the privilege of walking the paths of ancestors and learning the history of this once majestic stronghold.

I treasure my memories and my reflections and insights into times gone by. At the same time, I watch and listen to those who stop and admire my presence. I would love to share tales with them as they ponder on all that I have seen.

CHOP, CHOP SUEY
By C.G. Harris

There's something about the heat that brings out the crazies. That was my first thought when Chen knocked around midday and entered with a dish of Chinese food. He laid it on my desk – but only after I'd taken my feet off it.

The fan in the corner had been fooling around with the air since nine and the temperature was still rising; I'm guessing had the food been fresh cooked the smell may have stirred me – although during the day I'm a pastrami-on-rye kind of guy – but cold Chinese leaves me…cold. That aside, it shook me out of my 1949 Manhattan summer stupor; first, because Chen is the doorman down below and seeing him on the second floor is damn rare, and second, a severed pinkie finger sat on a bed of beef, vegetables, and rice.

I was surprised, but I ain't squeamish; I tried a cheap crack. "Off duty today, Chen? Is that a No.16 with extras?"

Chen was young and smart; inscrutable too, as you might expect – though I thought I caught a twitch of the lips. "You pretty damn good detective, Mr. Baum. That pretty damn right, yes?"

"Investigator, Chen. Private."

He bowed low and I raised an eyebrow. I was starting to get his oriental humor, sardonic for the most part. "What's the story, Chen?

He bowed again, more a nod this time. "Zhang Wei is friend of honorable father. Owner of most best restaurant on Pell Street; to dine at his restaurant last night was great honor and to accept hospitality also. Food top notch until chop suey arrive." He nodded at the dish. The finger was starting to look pretty down at heel. But not as bad as I thought it would after 14 hours or so.

"On top like that? I figure you've had it in the fridge overnight?"

"Yes, Mr. Baum, straight away. Detective stories reading at desk below, full of useful information. No, finger hidden under delicious gravy."

I said I wasn't squeamish, but that made me shiver a little. I got serious. "This is for the police, Chen. Have you phoned the cops? Someone's hurting or being hurt." I looked at the finger again. "Badly."

"No, Mr. Baum."

I reached for the phone; Jastrow at NYPD was going to love this one.

"No, Mr. Baum. No police, please."

I stopped. "Waddya mean?"

"Mr. Wei most insistent. Took all my...persuasive?" He got it wrong but I was listening. "To allow me to show you." Chen leaned towards me; the strict parting in his queued, long black hair stared right at me. "I think Mr. Wei frightened, Mr. Baum." He lifted his eyes to mine and his inscrutability had given way to something else. Alarm, perhaps. "Most frightened."

I pulled my arm back from the phone and looked at him, then the finger, and stood up. Chen looked small and worried at my six feet two, short hair and sweating shirt.

"Get some ice, wrap it up and bring it with you. And get rid of the food." I reached for my tie, then shrugged and left it there, limp, on the back of the chair. "Let's go see Mr. Wei."

*

The borders of Chinatown in downtown Manhattan are somewhat fluid; I don't visit much but the heart of it, the old town, is still around Mott and Pell Streets. Each of these is a riot of restaurants and you can find New Yorkers with chopsticks in hand at all times of day and night. From what

I've seen, most times chopsticks ain't good enough, because they can't spade the food in quick enough.

Chen and I took the subway to Canal Street and pushed our way through a crowded sidewalk. It was lunch and the heat was stopping no one; it had opened just a month ago but the Golden Dragon on Pell was busy. From the outside it looked gaudy, colorful, and exciting, though no more than the rest, but Chen had assured me on the way it had the best cuisine. I couldn't help thinking about the finger, but kept my mouth shut.

When we entered noise, heat, steam and aromas hit us hard. I'll give it to Zhang Wei, the smells were such that if I hadn't seen what Chen put on my desk, I'd have ordered something right off myself. I decided to stick to business. Though strictly it wasn't, of course; there was no client and, worse, no one was paying me. I sighed; it wasn't the first time I'd been a *schmuck*. Rabbi Jakob had told me enough times.

Chen looked around for Zhang Wei. We saw him looking harassed, but business was flowing and he was fussing at the waiters, who clattered quite efficiently from table to table. Did he look worried about what had happened? I didn't think so, but I couldn't tell from here. It was only when he saw us that he frowned and his eyes moved from side to side. He waved us over and we followed him through some saloon doors and upstairs to a small office with a window that looked out over the patron floor. He drew the blinds on that and we sat on hard bamboo chairs around a table of the same wood. A teapot and cups, decorative as hell, stood on it.

Zhang didn't look too happy when he found out who I was – his lined face puckered and his horseshoe moustache drooped – but Chen told him it was either the cops or me.

"Mr. Baum such good. If you are in trouble, he is the man for help."

I was flattered – but I think that was what he intended.

Zhang loosened up a little and I could see that he was more worried than he wanted to let on. His English was not so good and Chen decided it was better for him to ask Zhang what I wanted to know.

Investigating ain't so difficult, you know. The big question you want an answer to is: *Why?* If you can get something from that, you are halfway there. Sometimes you can only get to that if you think about: *How?* I started with that. Chen chattered away while I looked at my nails. Then Zhang chattered back.

"Okay, Mr. Baum. There is choices," Chen said.

"Uh huh?"

"There is chef. Mr.Wei knows him loo-ong time. Kitchen helper young, new. Three waiters, one Mr. Wei bring with him from last restaurant in Queens district and two hire recently." He paused. "Then there are plenty customers, of course."

I considered what he had told me, then asked Chen to take out the finger and unwrap it. It was messy, but not enough that we couldn't see it was small, dainty, with nails only a girl or a woman would have. Zhang stiffened. His eyes opened a little wider. But by the time Chen had asked him in Cantonese if there was any small chance he would know who it belonged to, he had closed up again. I got the feeling he was hiding something, but I couldn't be sure. I started feeling mean.

"Go on Mr. Wei, have a good look." I nodded for Chen to push it closer, right over to Zhang, who felt compelled to quickly move his hands away. I pretended not to notice the small tattoo under the wide sleeve of his cheongsam. A dragon and five red dots. "No? Okay." I stood up, and Chen alongside me. "I figure your staff are too busy to talk right now." I smiled like a wolf. "I'll be back in time for dinner."

When Chen translated that, Zhang looked pretty unhappy. Terrified, in fact.

*

I wondered how long I could hold off calling Jastrow at the precinct; it was crazy not to. I was back at the office and I thought about the finger I'd put in the corner fridge. Wrapped, sure, but I didn't like the idea it was mixing with the beer I had on ice; at least I'd kept it away from any comestibles. Jastrow would go nuts when he found out. There was only one thing stopping me...the look on Zhang's face. He was scared...I mean *scared*...of...? Whatever, it was enough for him not to tell the cops of something that was more than disturbing, it was sinister and frightening. It wasn't just about ruining his business – someone, somewhere was in big trouble. But this was my figuring; that I could get further forward than a huddled swathe of cops questioning opaque Orientals. If they don't want you to know something, you stayed not knowing.

Chen and I had swayed and sweated it back on the subway; those commuting alongside were bored, hot and irritable, but at least untroubled by enigmas. When we arrived, we sat in perspiring thoughtfulness for a while.

Then I started right in. "How long have you known Mr. Wei?"

"Met sometimes with my father, Mr. Baum. Chef too. Father is friend of Mr. Wei from Kwangtung many years."

I opened my appointment diary; it was pretty blank. On one of the pages, I drew as best I could a picture of a small dragon and five dots. "What's this?"

Chen took his time replying, but was honest enough. I already knew what it was. "It's a tong tattoo, Mr, Baum. Hip Sing Tong."

"He doesn't strike me as the type."

42

"Oh, he no criminal." He looked thoughtful." At least, I no think so. You must remember, Mr. Baum, that tongs are there for Chinese community."

"Was that before they went into pimping, drugs and the protection racket?"

Chen grimaced. "Ok, Mr. Baum, you are right. There are bad people in tongs. That is why father live quiet life now, not here. Far away."

"Ok. I won't ask where. This is the thing, Chen. I believe Zhang knows exactly why there's a finger in the food and who it belongs to. He may not know how it got there, but I'll figure that one out myself. Where does this all take us?" I pulled at my collar and undid another button. An uninvited fly took one look in the open window, didn't like what it saw and decided things were better elsewhere.

Chen shook his head and stood. His striped suit still looked unsullied in the heat; he was smart and modern, despite the long hair.

"I'll collect you at four," I said. "I need you."

He left, closing the door behind him. Even in leather shoes, his soft tread was such that it wouldn't have broken rice paper.

When he'd gone, I thought about what I knew, what I figured, then about all the things I didn't know in the world.

*

We reached the Golden Dragon an hour before opening.

In the room overlooking the restaurant, Zhang was looking less traditional and more business-like in a suit much like Chen's. He appeared just as worried, but politely poured us some tea anyhow; at my request, he then called down for each of the staff to attend us. I heard the first steps on the stairs, and I wondered whether I should play the tough cop role as I did when in the NYPD. Then I remembered I hated that, all that I hated about the force, and all the reasons I had got out. I didn't exactly smile then, but I kept a face with as little hostility on it as possible.

The chef looked traditional in a white, double-breasted work jacket but with no head covering. He looked puzzled, but half-bowed to Chen and then smiled at Zhang, who nodded and smiled back. It was clear these two were buddies and went back a long way, albeit Zhang was the boss. Chen translated as we went, but the conversation was along these lines.

"Yi Ming," said Chen. "Most sorry to take you from your duties. Mr. Baum, he is…friend…and would wish to ask you questions."

"Oh? Questions?"

"Sure," I said. I laid straight in. "You recall Chen at dinner here last night?"

He smiled. "Of course. I know Chen long time. I hope food was to satisfaction."

"Not exactly."

His face fell. "Most sorry, Chen. If disappointed, I will cook special meal for you. Allow me-"

"It was special enough, Mr. Ming." He looked puzzled again. It was time to tell him what Chen had found. His eyes went as round as Chinese plates and he goggled at Zhang. "Any ideas, Mr. Ming?"

"Mr Wei!"

Zhang held up his hand, then looked at me. "No more, Mr. Baum. Yi Ming cook for me since…ever so long. No more, please."

I shrugged then said quietly, "You say nothing, Mr. Ming, understand?" The tough guy came out; I just couldn't help it.

Ming nodded and bowed, looked anxiously at Zhang. Then he retreated. His steps seemed slower and heavier than they were on the way up.

We sat in silence while I gave things some thought. Chen was looking at me like I had all the answers; I didn't. Only one person did and he wasn't talking: Zhang, who was miserable, wringing his hands like a washer woman. He didn't want me here. That was tough.

"Get the others up here, one at a time," I growled. "And no finger talk."

We shifted through the staff and my questions were such that I could have been a disgruntled customer talking about a fly in the corn crab soup. They all looked worried, perhaps at losing their jobs, but *someone* put the finger in the suey and I figured I was experienced enough to spot guilt when I saw it.

The kitchen hand, Liu, was young and, by the end of questioning, I began to think simple.

Of the three waiters, the one who had come with Zhang from his restaurant in Queens was docile and I didn't like to see it; I much preferred the attitude of the other two. They had joined in the last month, were less nervous. In particular, Dingxiang gave me the sort of look that said he didn't give a damn. *'So, fire me,'* he seemed to be saying. Of course, he didn't know we were talking about detached fingers – or did he? – and aggravated assault or worse. I saw no tattoos.

When we were alone again, I gave it one more try with Zhang. I was as polite as I could be but I guess my frustration showed and my patience was wearing thin. "Is there anything you want to tell me, Mr. Wei? I can't help you if you don't."

Both Chen and I looked at him. For a moment, I thought it was all coming out. Then he trembled and bowed his head.

We both stood and then left, Zhang sitting with his head in his hands. I guessed I had no choice now but to tell the cops – but something was holding me back. It was the

45

thought that if I did, something real bad was going to happen.

*

Chen had left for home, wherever that was. I realised I did not know too much about him, but I knew from instinct that he was one of the good guys. Apart from when he had been an item with Rosie Vitalis along the corridor; I'd originally had ideas in that direction myself. Still, I don't hold that against him.

We had spent an hour or so back at the office tossing around what we knew and what we should do. Chen had agreed with me that Zhang knew who the finger belonged to. We couldn't agree on why he wouldn't go to the cops; it was a warning about something, that didn't take too much to work out, but it could be a lot more. My figuring was this: if it belonged to someone he cared about, he didn't want it to get worse.

I asked Chen about the tongs and when he told me about the On Leong that clicked with me. The Hip Sing and the On Leong weren't exactly bosom buddies; they weren't always the benevolent societies some believed either, but big players in previous tong wars. Where money and power are involved, benevolence takes a back seat – and morals too. Dope peddling, gambling, and sex trafficking; it's easy to make money from the weakness and desires of others.

I told Chen to call it a day. I hung around some time, thinking, and finally made up my mind the On Leong Merchants' Association seemed to be where this was leading. It made sense, but something about it didn't feel right; something more than just a bitter or murderous rivalry.

I shook my head and decided to head home to La Salle; I was a little surprised to find that somehow the evening had closed into night and I was sitting in the dark.

46

Before closing up, I stood at the window and looked out over Manhattan. The city that never sleeps was still bold, bright, and busy; the sounds of traffic told me so, and the lights, and the smells. I tried to imagine the vanilla smell of Upper East Side, the perfume of Soho, the side-cart nuts and pretzels of 5th. But all I got were auto fumes and garbage; and still I loved it.

*

La Salle can be a crowded street. They could have chosen better places to jump me, but I guess when I was looking for my block keys with my head down was as good as any. I guess the plan was to push me inside and hustle me up to my apartment before beating me, or worse.

I had subwayed to 125th with my body losing sweat and my mind still full. A three-minute walk to La Salle and I was looking forward to a cold beer and a burger when I felt something slim and hard against the small of my back. It could have been a gun barrel but my best guess was the blade of a knife; silent and unobtrusive. Without turning around, I couldn't tell how many there were but it would not be one, I knew. I also knew that once I was inside, I was lost.

They wouldn't have known I was a veteran. Pacific, two-year term, heat, blood, death. I didn't like to think about it too much, but once learned the things that kept you alive never go away – in my line of business I give thanks for that often.

So, I fought. I pushed back and heard someone stumble on the steps and someone else curse. I guess it was a curse because it was in Chinese. I turned and at the same time struck out twice with 220 pounds behind each blow. When I saw there were three of them, I knew I was going to get hurt. Two of them had clubs, the other a knife – these were the *boo how doy*, soldiers of the tongs, so Chen had told me; dumb and uneducated, but precise in what they were required to do – that is, beat, maim, or kill.

If it hadn't been for Rabbi Jakob, I think I would have seen my last chop suey; the one thing I would have been grateful for. As it was, I had grabbed the one with the knife while the others beat me in the face and arms and I was sinking to my knees when I heard a shout: "*Oy vey!* What is this! What is this!"

One further blow to my face and they scurried away like so many spiders, blacker than the night and, it seemed, with more legs and arms than anybody should have.

"Tscchh! Aaron, Aaron, come, come." The rabbi was kind and strong. I'd forgotten how many times he had been there for me, for my dying *ima*, my mama long gone.

In my apartment, the rabbi sat me down in the chair I loved best, the high-backed one with the unfashionable stripes, and poured me a scotch; he looked for a little wine himself and poured a smidgeon. I could feel my face swelling and he found a cloth, wrapped some ice in it and made me hold it to my jaw.

"Now. Aaron, what…?"

It was difficult to speak, but I told him. I could always talk to Jakob. His lined, wise face peered right at me. "Now is the time to speak to Mr. Jastrow, is it not?"

I nodded and he passed me the telephone. Jastrow would be at home, but it wouldn't be the first time I had called him late; he knew what trouble was and it didn't keep office hours.

He picked up the call. "Jastrow. Make it brief."

"It's Baum."

"Baum? What's that, you say? *Oy,* you sound like you're chewing on a mouthful of teeth."

I sighed and tried again. "What do you know about tongs?" At least, I think it came out like that.

*

When you finally make firm decisions, things can happen quickly. Firstly, Jastrow called round to my apartment early next morning. He was as tall and brown and tough as the last time I'd seen him; at a homicide, as it happens. I laid it all out to him as best I could with a swollen jaw and aching ribs. We figured out what was now an obvious thing – that someone Zhang cared about (daughter? not wife, surely) was being held by a rival tong, probably the On Leong. No idea why, but who could figure the oriental mind? Jastrow pointed out to me that the reasons for brutal actions by gangs were usually the same: money, control, power, occasionally revenge.

We needed Zhang to speak to us to let us know whether we had got it right and to let *him* know that we had it in hand. He was scared, of course, terrified that if the On Leong knew he had gone to the cops there would be something worse in the chop suey and he would never see whoever it was again.

First question – how the hell would we find where she was held?

The second – I couldn't figure why he hadn't got the Hip Sing to help him. Perhaps the same thing applied – that if he made any contact, it was bamboo curtains.

It was then that it hit me. When I had asked myself: *'Why?'* I hadn't got it quite right. It should have been: *'Why Chen?'*

Let me reason it out.

If anyone else had found that finger in their food they would have gone straight to the cops – after getting a refund, naturally. To send a message but not get the cops involved meant serving it to someone who would only go to Zhang; that was Chen. Who knew Chen? Who else knew

49

he would be at the restaurant that night? Only Yi Ming. Good old Yi Ming – faithful friend and chef to Zhang Wei.

Let me go further.

Although Zhang didn't know how the finger got there, he knew who had arranged it – and it was the reason he couldn't turn to the Hip Sing for help. It was them, not the On Leong. Yeah, my mind was turning over quick now, and it felt good. Zhang had fallen foul of the Hip Sing and the lesson was: we can ruin your business, or we can hurt the ones you love – or we can do both. I didn't have all the answers, or even all the questions – but it felt right what I had. Jastrow would confirm it all quietly with Zhang. There was only one thing more, the important thing: how do we get back safely whoever owned that finger?

*

The Golden Dragon finally closed, late. The streets around were still busy but the atmosphere changed from hustling, bustling working class to that of subtle debauchery. I had the idea that, in among the hard-working regular businesses, there were some that, behind closed doors, turned to something else when dark fell; I'd heard that parts of Chinatown were called the City's Mistress.

I don't know if we were unobtrusive or not while we were waiting for Yi Ming to leave, but we did our best. There were still plenty of cars parked and I was with Chen in my old grey Chevy that passed everyone's notice by; it may once have had class, but no more. Jastrow and his buddy from Precinct 14 were in a black Buick and I knew he was in contact with the station if back up was needed. Who knew what to expect – but it would be trouble, for sure. In my pocket I had a solid black-jack that had served me well in times of trouble; it had cracked the heads of many low-lives.

Jastrow had got a message to Zhang through Chen about what we were going to do: follow Yi Ming. We figured that after my dusting with the *boo how doy* they would make some kind of nasty move that involved whoever they were holding.

Chen told me that Zhang nearly fainted when he told him - and it all came tumbling out. He confirmed, yeah, the Hip Song had his niece. Following his success with the restaurant – started up with a loan from them – they wanted to use him as a front for illicit stuff. He was okay up to a point. When they told him they were moving into sex trafficking, that was too much for him. But once you are in, neck-wise, it ain't so easy to get out of the noose; he'd been a member long enough to know that.

Yi Ming, he counted as a friend and would not believe he had anything to do with it. In his defence, I guessed that Ming had no choice either; the Hip Sing gave him the finger – literally – and special chop suey was put on the menu.

I didn't know it, but the Manhattan headquarters of the Hip Sing Association was at number 15, just a couple of hundred yards along Pell Street from the restaurant. I shook my head when I found out; no wonder Zhang was scared under that baleful eye. When Yi Ming came out of the restaurant, I was expecting him to head that way – but he didn't.

He was dressed in a smart striped suit – it looked grey under the lights, but could have been brown – with a waistcoat, white shirt, and tie. He had a fedora pulled low over his brows and he hurried away in the direction of Doyer Street, then hailed a cab. We followed. The traffic hadn't let up too much; it was gone eleven, but it was Friday and it was time for the put-upon and the high rollers alike to take pleasure in what they will. I hoped they had all had time for a shower, but I didn't think it would make much difference; the night was still warm enough to make a lizard sweat.

The cab crawled around the streets for ten minutes or so and finally pulled over opposite a three-story building that flashed neon in primary colours above the door – it aspired to be classy and was trying but failing. The sign said Club Nanjing and had a poster full of Oriental girls – all beautiful, fish-netted up, smiling. Chen told me that it was a downmarket version of the China Doll on 51st street, where patronising whites watched a cabaret of singing, dancing Chinese and Vietnamese as they had once watched Blacks at the Cotton Club.

We could hear music but couldn't make it out. At the door, a queue of men, the occasional dame, were decked out in weekend finery. Most of the men were balding and filled their suits to the limit. A white guy, looking tough but none too bright, checked their credentials before nodding them in. Yi Ming was stopped, exchanged a few words, and was waved through.

I watched Jastrow and one of his cop buddies get out of their car. They weren't too shabby in their plain clothes, respectable even, but no tie, and headed towards the door. He looked towards me and I followed, with Chen in tow.

The guy on the door was as tall as both Jastrow and myself, bigger round the chest but also the gut, and hooded his eyes as we approached,

"Help you?" he said.

"Yeah," growled Jastrow. "We'd like to see the show."

"No entry without a ticket or an invitation."

Jastrow flashed his badge. "Good enough?"

The guy's eyes opened a little wider and while he was making up his mind Jastrow, his sidekick – name of Hicks – Chen and I brushed him aside. I kept my head down; a swollen jaw and bruising didn't lend itself to matching the normal clientele. From the corner of my eye, I saw another guy of the same build and no doubt intellect moving off to the side; I figured he was taking the news to whoever was in charge.

That happened to be a guy called Bobby Liu. I know, because thirty seconds later he stood in front of us. He was smoother than a grasshopper cocktail in a tuxedo, black with white shirt, bow tie and a hint of cuff at the sleeves. The show had already started and the music was heady and swinging. A trio of beautiful Chinese girls in stockings swayed on stage and sang harmony to a popular song I couldn't put a name to, and a score of round tables were filled with the fat and the not so famous; they were all being served with spirits and wine by equally alluring girls of Oriental extraction. Spotlights cut an occasional swathe through cigarette smoke rising from puckered lips and ashtrays. One thing I noticed further: guys were sidling to tables and dealing soft drugs to laughing clientele. I drew Jastrow's attention with a nudge. The fact was, we didn't have a warrant and we needed a lever. In the meanwhile, Chen was eyeballing the room for a sign of Ming.

"Gentlemen, can I help you?" Bobby Liu was polite, though his smile was cold as ice. I wondered whether he was Hip Sing or had just been financed by them.

"Sure," said Jastrow. "We're looking for someone."

"Anyone in particular? By the way, do you have a warrant?"

"Would you like me to get one?" Jastrow nodded in the direction of a guy passing a small packet to a guy who looked like he could do with losing a few pounds; I figured with the weight, the drugs, and the excitement of the scantily clad, he may not last the night.

Liu didn't even move his eyes, just shrugged. "Be my guest."

We moved around the room; it was hard not to do it to the beat of the music and even harder not to look out of place. There was no sign of Ming.

It was Chen who found the staircase. He'd been drawn to a small kitchen to the side and, pushing through the doors, saw steps leading up to a door that looked solid and out of place. It had opened abruptly, and a scared-looking Ming looked out. His mouth fell open and he backed away as soon as he saw Chen.

"Mr Baum!"

I heard Chen shout and burst my way into the kitchen. Two Chinese guys wearing white work jackets and mean looks stood there barring our way. They had cleavers – and I didn't think they were used just for preparing meals. Jastrow pushed past me, pulled his gun, and waved it at them. He ain't patient, is Jastrow. One of the guys raised his arm and Jastrow shot that same arm. Blood spurted, and for some reason I was thinking how hard it was going to be cleaning up that kitchen. Then I ran for the staircase door. I could hear a scream or two from the patron floor at the sound of the gunshot; I was pleased it had ruined their night.

It was a tough door, but Hicks and I kicked and shouldered it and it crashed open. More stairs and more screams – this time from above. Each scream gave us a fresh sense of urgency and we reached the top of a second flight breathless. A guy at the top cursed us in Chinese – I wondered whether it was the same one who had beaten up on me a couple of days ago. That made me mad and before he could say or do anymore, I sapped him with the black-jack and stepped over him – I decided not to kick him when he was down. We rattled open another door. What we saw made me madder still.

Four young women – I won't call them girls, though they weren't far from it – lay or sat on sofas. They looked doped up, to be honest, scared but quiet, apart from the one who was screaming who had a scuffed and soiled bandage around her hand. All were Chinese but dressed in western clothes. Ming stood mute in the corner with his hands in the air. Two other guys rushed us – Jastrow shot them both. That was the way he dealt with those he thought were scum.

*

Things were quiet. I unravelled the remaining knots the following day over a beer (Jastrow) and tea (Chen).

Ming had been arrested for procuring girls and whatever putting decaying fingers in food might come under. He wasn't charged with kidnapping; that wasn't him, but the tong and nailing anyone at the top wasn't going to be easy. He wasn't talking too much; he valued his life.

Here's where it becomes a little scary – for me. Bobby Liu's club had been closed down by the cops. Chen told me that the Hip Sing weren't too happy with me. I had not heard of the shadowy Huang, head of the tong, and I pictured someone with a Fu Manchu moustache, but Jastrow showed me a photograph from the files. He had slick black hair, western-style clothes, and a smile as he played Mahjong with some buddies. In a second photo, he was looking directly into the camera. I didn't like the dead fish eyes. I thought I might have trouble some dark night.

That evening, I strolled one more time along Pell Street. It was still busy, but not at the Golden Dragon; it was closed. For good, I imagined. Zhang was wanted, and not in a good way; I hoped he had found the quiet life that Chen's father had. Outside the shuttered restaurant were mouldering fish heads.

I walked on – and wondered why I still loved New York when it stank of rotting hopes and dreams.

For more Aaron Baum detective stories see "Murder in Manhattan – The Casebook of Aaron Baum" available on Amazon and www.cgharrisauthor.com *for that book and* others by this author.

A TRIP TO THE SEASIDE
By Jan Brown

Bob and Joan's seaside expeditions were legendary in the '70s. A whole gang of family, friends, neighbours, and hangers-on had gone along to Hastings, usually on motorbikes, a number with sidecars. Some neighbourhoods in Hastings greeted the visitors with delight, others with derision, but Big Bob and Juicy Joan (a nickname bestowed on her by Bob for her love of Kia Ora juice) had no cares; they loved life.

Some fifty years later, the gang had either got old or died. Motorbikes were out and coach travel was in, with the remainder of the gang favouring Starlight Coaches as they had three toilets – and, more importantly, two of these were downstairs for the less able-bodied; a useful addition for the journey to Hastings on this, a warm July day.

"All off, we've arrived," the driver shouted loudly, having skilfully parked the coach in a spot that didn't look big enough for the vehicle. He stood by the open door, ostensibly to assist anyone with shaky legs to disembark but also taking the opportunity to have a crafty fag and jiggle his 'tip' bucket hopefully in every passenger's face.

The bed and breakfast residence favoured by what remained of the original gang had no en-suite facilities. It was cheap but not particularly cheerful. In one room, age and disenchantment had inevitably raised its head.

"Must you wear that bright pink stretchy stuff, Joanie?" For his part, in his senior years Bob had gravitated easily to a more muted approach with regards his clothing and outlook.

"What's up with you, you boring old git?" returned Joanie, slashing 'Hot Pink Babe' lipstick over her thin cracked lips. She puckered up. "Give us a kiss."

"Huh." Bob moved impressively swiftly to the left, avoiding the oncoming assault, then shuffled off towards the shared bathroom. "You look like an uncooked sausage in that get-up."

"Bloody cheek." Joan peered at her blurry image in the mirror. "At least I'm not all doom and gloom."

The following day quickly warmed up, turning into a scorcher. A brilliant blue sky hung over the packed beach, a hue so perfect it seemed painted on; an idyllic backdrop for the children making sandcastles and the adults enjoying sand-infused butties. The sea was calm and alluring as it lapped gently at the ankles of paddlers.

Bob and Joan sat on their rented deckchairs, the former's thin, white, hairy legs standing out starkly against the thick red and blue stripes. Joan stood up abruptly and stared down at her husband snoring on, his lips blowing in and out; the nose hairs that hung down from his left nostril quivered in concert and she wrinkled her own nose gently in disgust.

The children's laughter suddenly sounded distant to Joan and she felt removed from reality, as if she were a spectator or an observer to events outside her control. She continued to watch Bob as he slept on and didn't disturb him when the tide began to wash in, the crowds of sun seekers and excited children gathering and heading off for burgers, pizza or fish and chips.

The beach was silent now as twilight fell; the sea took on a harsh greyness and the wind began to whip up the waves. Bob slept on. Joan began to quietly gather her belongings together, the straw hat squashed into her M&S carrier bag on top of the bucket and spade she'd bought.

"What on earth do you want those for, you stupid woman? Building sandcastles at your age!" Bob had shouted at her in the amusement arcade, causing hordes of teenagers to look, many to laugh and others to pity. It was, perhaps, the final straw.

Now, she told the first police officer to arrive: "I'd intended to bury him in the sand, you know. But I realised I'd never dig deep enough; the old bugger would have woken up anyway."

"Madam, you don't seem to appreciate the seriousness of your inaction. You allowed your husband to drift out to sea and drown. You could have alerted him at any point, called a lifeguard or even us and prevented this tragedy."

Joan smiled at the officer. "He looked so peaceful just drifting away."

She gazed out at the sea for some moments, past and present converging, then shivered and pulled up the zip of her bright pink tracksuit top.

"He was such a grey man, officer."

THE HOUSE BY THE RIVER
By Janet Winson

Tomorrow I'll be leaving my house by the river. For the last time, I will shut the door behind me then drop two sets of keys through the black cast-iron letter box.

The new owners will move in by two o'clock. By then I'll be having a cup of tea with Juliet and preparing my new home in her granny annexe.

Juliet's house is not by a river. It has a vista all its own; it sits near a large golf course and, from the suburbs of Halifax, looks out across the moors. Where my house is made of stone, nearly 150 years old now, the top windows extra-large as these houses were built for the weavers of the old town, Juliet's is neo-Georgian, a large house on a gated estate. I love my daughter and know I'm lucky to be wanted by her and her family, but there is this worry: that I leave my heart in my house by the river.

My original arrival here in Yorkshire fifty years past was dramatic and I had protested against it, but only inwardly. My husband of two years had been offered a job as sub-editor on the Rochdale Recorder – so we left our tiny flat in Stockwell and said goodbye to family, friends, and our jobs: his at the South London Press and mine as a teacher at Stockwell Infant School. We had only just discovered that there was a baby on the way, and although this job was a terrific chance for him, I cried for two months non-stop leading up to our departure.

In my early 20s I knew nothing of 'Oop North', Yorkshire particularly. All that I *did* know was taken from books, my childhood favourites: *Jane Eyre*, *Wuthering Heights*, and *The Secret Garden*. They all described a bleak and unwelcoming landscape with a good number of disagreeable characters to boot.

It was a long and distressing journey for me to this unknown town by the river, named for the bridge across it; I'd never heard of Hebden Bridge. The house itself was at first unlovely. A solid front door opened into a large, terraced home with plenty of room, but it was run down and dowdy. There was no central heating and dreadful pre-war plumbing; my heart sank and stayed in the vicinity of my Wellington boots for the first months.

The whole of my pregnancy was fraught with anxiety, alongside a feeling of bereavement for my old life. I was lonely and not well, physically. I felt pressured into trying to make a home in this strange, alien town. How I missed my family, friends, colleagues! My heart hung heavily within me; at the same time, I was being bruised from the inside.

The house needed a great deal of money spent on it. The first winter there was bitterly cold and with only a coal fire, which hardly kept the living room warm enough, I almost gave up all hope of making this a comfortable home and a life that I could cherish. However, as it always does, spring slowly came and the box room was transformed into a newly painted nursery with bright, fresh walls. I felt myself yielding to a new feeling of hope, and when my daughter Juliet arrived, life was better than I could have imagined. I fell in love with her so easily. The river and the town had begun to weave a little magic at last.

However, life slipped into a new phase now, and not a pleasant one. The early years of being a mother in a place that still did not truly feel like home began to forge a rift in my marriage. As he, the breadwinner, steadily gained promotion at work, I became increasingly aware of the difference between handing children back to their parents after school and the ever-present commitment of parenting. I also yearned to go back home to the south, to be with the people I knew. I wanted to laugh with my old friends, be surrounded by the places I knew and the atmosphere I had grown up in. I still saw my life as belonging to those infants in London. I recalled buttoning up their colourful winter woollies in the playground, settling warm hats on their heads, wrapping them up against the chill air.

A wet and grey summer became the worst of times as I became pregnant again before Juliet had even reached her second birthday. I could not accept this; I felt I had barely got to grips with motherhood and was madly paddling just to keep afloat. Black moods and lack of communication between us was increasingly alienating my husband and me, although life for him was good at this time, his work and social life taking off. When I heard he had joined the golf club it felt like the last straw for me. I was jealous and a domestic cold war was truly on my hands.

Ironically, the pregnancy that had never felt right came to a natural end at harvest time when I lost the baby. I felt no peace for many months and I comforted myself by imagining a return to London with Juliet, back to my roots, and giving up on this half-baked, gruelling project of a marriage. I was also aware that my husband had been seeing a woman at work, and I'm ashamed to admit this came as no surprise.

I continued to feel at odds with the way my life was flowing away. I wanted to make a dam and stop time passing so quickly, leaving this place and meandering to a calm haven where I could feel the sun again. I hoped this would give me the peace I was looking for and make my life free flowing and brim-full of good things but, ultimately, I felt guilty for thinking these things... I had a home and a duty to my child, but I knew things could not continue unaltered after an infidelity and I begged my husband to change his job; when he agreed, I felt this could be the beginning of a new chapter.

My energy was channelled into growing alongside Juliet as I pushed her towards new experiences and showed her the brilliance of the world around us. She grew to love the river, visiting the ducks most days, where I held her hand very tightly. She was my greatest treasure and my love grew daily.

I remember one dull, overcast day at the river's edge. Behind some dead water foliage, a beautiful swan came into view on the tail of a paddling of ducks. Above me, geese skeined the mottled sky, disappearing as quickly as they'd materialised. My mind was made up: I would stay. Over the next months, I felt my roots here growing deeper into the living soil; the path ahead was becoming clearer to me and with the arrival of my baby son in the dark winter months just after Christmas, a surer and happier phase of my life began after the stormy period. I became increasingly more settled and calmer in my soul.

Wandering down to the river, I would feed the ducks and watch the houseboats and brightly painted canal boats further along where the water met the old canal path. As the years passed, I began to identify myself with the river. There was the river every afternoon, in fine or filthy weather; a home to the ducks and various birds that come and go according to the season. Importantly, it was also a meeting place for old folk, young mothers, adolescents – and there was somewhere to buy a nice cup of tea and a slice of cake in one of the nearby cafes. It was a wonderful place to ruminate and observe not only the changing seasons but those people that enjoyed it with me.

In truth, the town changed as I reached my 40s, just as I had changed myself. As the older generation who had been born in this area of mills and woollen weaving, once known as "Trouser Town," started to move away or die, the whole town became a growing community of artisans and, as they established themselves, Hebden Bridge entered a new period in its development. Tourism blossomed, but none of this destroyed my love for the town; it had, and always will have, a traditional and unique atmosphere. The river was still a place of almost daily pilgrimage for me and I absorbed everything around me. Time truly disappeared, like blown cobwebs on a box hedge.

I look back now on fifty years. Seamlessly, my life has moved on little by little through the years. My house by the river has become too large for me and I have been living here quite alone for several years. The early death of my husband was a terrible time but the house and the river were a constant; they kept me going until I could look once more upon the morning sun and be glad. The children have matured, been educated, disappeared, returned, and finally gone on to create their own life stories.

I look out upon the hills, which are now too steep for me to walk and climb; I can't get out half as much as I'd like. I look out also upon the flooding waters, horrendous here for the last two winters. Juliet says it is no longer a suitable environment for me. She's a teacher, just as I once was, so I suppose she is right.

Tonight will be my last sleeping in the front bedroom with the wide, extra-big window. I will leave the curtains open and the windows ajar and for one final time I will savour the familiar sounds of this house and the murmur of the river by its side. My wish is that as I sleep, the memories of my years here will fill my dreams and leave me with an abiding peace.

Life, like my river, will take me on, come fair weather or foul.

PARALYSIS
By Houria Gheran

I am back in that black room, where I am all alone. What is more, I feel and hear the wind; it gives me goosebumps. *My god... it has returned.* There is only darkness in my mind and it is coming at me like a dementor with no clear face; but somehow the black mouth is even darker than all around it. I see it, wide open and coming towards me.

I am paralysed again; I cannot move my legs or arms. I try to send a signal to my limbs but it seems they are turned to stone.

Seriously, I don't need this happening at this moment in time... Please move, guys; I need your cooperation. This is madness. You are talking to your legs as if they have a heartbeat and are separate living beings. Snap out of it. Get your brain working – you need to find a way out of this.

But I have no luck because all of a sudden it is as if my brain has left the room and I can find no solution.

I watch this monster, with his flowing cloak, approach. I recognise him – because he has been pursuing me for months. Always at night.

I do not know why I am his prey; perhaps it is simply that I am about to become his dinner! What can I do to keep myself safe?

My fear paralyzes me. I cannot even move my eyes.

Let me try a prayer to save myself, as my mother once advised me when I was frightened as a child. I try; however, this time even prayer does not work. There is water on my face, and I realise tears are streaming from my eyes like droplets of rain.

Minutes pass – I cannot say how many. I still cannot move and this monster is now beside me. But there is a difference. I can finally feel something; my arms and legs are being held by shackles.

The darkness lifts enough to allow me to see movement at the corners of my eyes. I can see enough to know that they are not shackles after all… My tormentor has brought his minions. To eat me?

There are two trolls holding my left leg; two others are holding my right. Between them, they constrain my arms. Is this why I cannot move, after all?

There is more terror. A troll is on top of my head and he has a hammer. He raises it. He is banging it on my head. The thuds pulsate. This cannot be borne, and the darkness is descending once more – perhaps this time forever.

But I hear birds. The sound of wings. White doves are breaking through the suffocating gloom and coming towards me. The sound of their singing is relief.

It is now that I realise, I am in my own room. The birds are outside my window and I finally manage to awaken from the nightmare. But this time, it is different; when I fully wake, my head pounds and the thumping continues.

That stupid troll with his hammer…

DONNA THE DOLPHIN
By Richie Stress

Donna was a dolphin. Her friend Denise was also a dolphin.

"It's not as good as the Balm 7. It may last longer, but it's not as smooth," Donna clicked.

"Yeah, and I find it leaves little sticky patches on the skin. I'm sticking with the 7 for now," Denise replied as she expertly caught another fish and wolfed it down in a single gulp.

A television screen rose like a colossus out of the ocean and towered 100 metres square above the waterline.

"She's so fake—no one's skin is that amazing," Donna said as an advert for the new and improved dolphin moisturiser, Balm 7.1, played in a perpetual loop. The dolphin in the commercial was leaping around and performing somersaults under a perfect sky, her skin radiating in the twinkling sunlight.

*

It had been three years since humans had finally discovered an effective way to communicate with the species *Delphinus delphis*. Of course, the first thing they did was try to exploit this achievement for financial gain. The main problem was that, apart from not really producing anything, overall, the dolphins seemed to be pretty content with the life that fifty million years of evolution had provided. Their lifestyle was made up of three components: catching and eating fish, copulating with multiple partners, followed by periods of rest and sleep. It didn't take long for humans to create a fourth component, though—one the creatures obviously didn't know they needed.

And so, Dolphin-Friendly Moisturiser was invented, with the newly discovered economic demographic literally lapping it up—until someone mentioned you put it on your skin and not eat it!

The problem of what the dolphins could trade for this essential product was solved after much negotiation with the Worldwide Dolphin Corporation. The dolphins would power wind turbines by swimming in circles around a fixed point in the sea and rack up 'M Credits' for every circuit completed. They could then exchange these for vouchers to purchase moisturiser balm products. The energy created would power state-of-the-art satellites that could be used to further explore Dolphin-Man communications and telecommunications.

The one drawback, as far as the dolphins were concerned, was that they were now spending so much time and energy on getting vouchers that they had to sacrifice what they'd previously spent a third of their life doing—namely, having sex with multiple partners. The consequence of this was that most had reluctantly switched to a life of monogamy.

"How's your Derek?" enquired Donna.

"He's fine. Well, he's complaining I'm not satisfying him enough…but then look at it this way: only 500 more circuits, and I'll have enough vouchers to keep us and the kids in Balm 7 until well after Christmas," Denise clicked.

The sound from another almost identical advert boomed out of the massive speakers above them.

"Oh, sorry, I forgot—you never adopted Christmas, did you, Donna?" continued Denise.

"I'm tired," clicked Donna. "I miss the old days."

EXPEDITION TO THE POLE 2006
By Tony Ormerod

The call came midweek. It was cricket secretary Brian Jones. Trying not to appear too keen, yet failing, I hastened into the lounge and almost snatched the telephone from my wife's hand. She gave me one of her 'isn't it time you gave that silly game up?' looks, which I pretended not to notice.

"How are you?" he enquired. He always did begin any conversation courteously by checking on my fitness, fully aware that I would shortly be receiving the first installment of my old age pension and surely something must have gone physically wrong; something must be ailing me. I assured him that all was well, and we got down to business.

"There's a game," he announced with a hint of triumph in his voice - arranging friendly games through the Fixture Bureau was not always easy – "but I'm not sure if you'll want to play!"

"Of course I'll play," I replied, unthinkingly. No prima donna I and, in any case, it was already halfway into the season and scorers had remained untroubled by my contributions with both bat and ball. Inevitably, sadly, my cricketing career was tottering to an end.

"It's against a team called Clapham Wanderers." After a short pause, he added, "and the match is in Kingston."

"On Thames?" I asked. Privately, I was hoping that perhaps there was another one a bit closer to home. If not, why were Clapham playing so far away from their own patch?

"Yes, I'm afraid it is." I detected a giggle as he added, "And it's in a park."

Oh great, I thought, doggie deposits on the pitch, uninvited members of the public strolling all over the place, getting in the way! Naturally, I remained upbeat and, even though I suspected that my selection had more to do with car ownership than my prowess on the field of play, I agreed to meet up at Sidhurst Sports Club on the Saturday at 11:30 am.

The night before my comeback, wife Christine and I dined well at our good friends the Griggs's place. It was not an ideal preparation for the following day. Driving into Sidhurst on that murky Saturday morning, I consoled myself with these thoughts: 1. We had twelve men, so I would volunteer to do the decent thing by simply umpiring. 2. Someone else could surely fit me into their car? Lastly, and importantly 3. There would be no game; it was bound to rain, and very soon.

I was sadly mistaken on all counts. Secretary Brian was already in the car park issuing instructions to drivers and it was he who disabused me of any plans I may have had with regard to umpiring and/or travelling as a passenger. Someone had selfishly dropped out. "Are you still here, Tone?" was his way of hastening my departure. I had hung around praying for rain.

For a few moments, out of consideration for my fragile condition following the previous evening's excesses, Hugh Chomley - Webb offered to drive my car. My relief was short-lived when he, quite rightly, switched effortlessly into solicitor mode by having second thoughts about the insurance situation. He was appointed navigator and, clutching my deluxe *A to Z*, he took his place beside me. Occupying the back seats were Jim Patel and young Tim Roberts. With me, reluctantly, at the wheel, we set off on our adventure. It was 11:45 am. By the time we reached the first crossroad the rest of the convoy had been shaken off. However, as we approached the dreaded M25 it became increasingly obvious that the weather was not the only thing that was closing in on us. Call it instinct but I just knew it was going to end badly. Crawling along the M25 bumper to bumper on a miserable Saturday afternoon with a weather-doomed cricket match to get to… Why were we bothering? Fortunately, Hugh was on hand to provide some of the answers. His wide range of topics included optimism, pessimism, and defeatism. Jim Patel weighed in with, for example, "Who is the best batsman/bowler you have ever seen?"

Our two hours on the motorway seemed to fly by. Young Tim's contributions to our in-car entertainment were "When are we going to get there?" and "I'm bored." He would be an old fart himself in the far-off future. Where was that rain?

Any faint hopes of reaching our destination in time for the scheduled 2 pm start had faded even before we finally limped off the M25, a situation made worse when we found ourselves heading away from Kingston rather than towards it. A mere ten-minute diversion, we were at least in the right county. I had never been a fan of the Kingston one way system, having, back in the sixties, spent what seemed to be an entire afternoon trying to escape from it. Now, fate's fickle finger was beckoning me back. My navigator, compelled to leave the vehicle for a conference with pedestrians, jabbed away at my map book and quickly ascertained that we were quite close to where we wanted to be. One stranger, Hugh said, had wondered if my deluxe *A to Z* might be out of date. Cheek! That bumper edition of an excellent publication had served me well for over twenty years. Surely Kingston had not changed that much? I felt that it mattered little what the age of one's map was. None of them seemed to indicate clearly where a road had been closed off to through traffic, on the whim of selfish residents and compliant borough engineers, bent on denying access to visiting drivers desperately trying to reach their objectives. It was a conspiracy!

Our predicament was not helped by the phone call that Hugh elected to take on his 'mobile.' I thought things could not get worse, but they did. Our navigator calmly chatted away with what I could only assume was a close relative on urgent family business, just when I needed him most. Egged on vocally by Messrs.' Patel and Roberts, turning the wheel this way and that, somehow, at the moment Hugh terminated his call, we arrived at our destination! I hesitated to think critically of a former Sidhurst captain (one of nature's gentlemen) but towards the end, perhaps unfairly, I thought we had arrived in spite of, rather than because of his navigational skills.

A posse of traffic wardens was swarming. What was that, a training exercise? There was no obvious vehicular entrance into the park. Here was another fine mess, I thought. Unreasonably, out loud, I enquired of my passengers: "Why didn't our secretary tell us about this?" Peering through the windscreen, noting that it should be pouring with rain any minute, I could barely make out white-clad figures moving about in the misty conditions. The opposition! It was now 2:45 pm. Pete Evans, our captain for the day, appeared still in his 'civvies', and, leaving our cars to their fate, we approached one of the traffic wardens who was energetically carrying out his duties. Nevertheless, a decent fellow, he pointed out that we should try to use a small parking area in the school adjacent to the park. It was only as we, using four cars, drove in that we spied a notice warning us that trespassing vehicles would be clamped. Furthermore, the gates to the totally empty car park could be locked by caretaking staff. How could it be so dark and threatening yet so dry?

I forget now whose good idea it was to 'station guards' at the entrance on quarter hour watches, on a rota basis, and hopefully with the full cooperation and participation of our hosts. We Sidhurst players approached the playing area, noting with satisfaction that we could just about see our cars from what could laughingly be called 'the pitch', and we were met by our concerned opponents and two men armed with huge spades who appeared to be digging a pit next to a large metal pole.

"It's no good, lads," said one of them, removing a dangerously small cigarette from his lips, "it won't budge." His companion concurred with that assessment. From their dress, we correctly placed them as Kingston on Thames employees.

The grey metal post, protruding from the turf, standing at least four feet above it and roughly six by six inches square, remained defiantly and merely ten yards from a set of stumps. It was one of half a dozen which, roped together, had ostensibly kept the general public at bay. Both teams and the two defeated workmen stood and stared at it. Someone muttered: "Health and safety." Naturally we eleven men of Sidhurst CC were not going to stand for that sort of nonsense, having gone through so much aggravation to get to our destination. It was 3 pm, and as the men with spades slowly withdrew, we explained our reasons for our lateness to the Wanderers.

Sympathetic towards our problem, they admitted that they had only played once on the park themselves. A small, distinguished-looking man, sporting a neat goatee beard, separated himself from the rest and introduced himself as their captain. "Hif der ball heet zer pole eet vill be dead," he kept repeating.

Those of us who understood nodded our agreement. Some wag asked, "What if we hit it?" A fair point.

It was as we were being led to the changing facility that I managed to have a quick word with one of our opponents, for I was intrigued by the strong, unusual accent of his skipper. It was reminiscent, I thought, of Bela Lugosi in the film *Dracula*; 'Pleasant dreams, der children of der night' etc. "Do I detect," I enquired, "a trace of Eastern European in your captain's voice?"

"Yes," he replied, guiding me towards a modest, very small but solid brick-built utility council building. "He's from Bulgaria."

Not then from Transylvania, but close. "A bit unusual, that," said I, laughing lightly, "having a Bulgarian skipper."

He became thoughtful. "Well, no. Ivan plays chess!" A strange qualification for cricket captaincy, it seemed to me, but it was different. No official umpires presided.

Captains Pete and Ivan agreed on a much-reduced match of 35 overs per side in view of the various hold-ups and an ever-worsening gloom that enveloped the park. We batted first but I did not get changed into my whites immediately, electing instead to umpire on a temporary basis as Hugh and Mat Edwards opened our innings on a pitch that looked as though it had never been introduced to a roller. In fact, frankly, there was little to distinguish the pitch from the rest of the cricket field. I thought I felt a drop of rain as Captain Ivan opened the bowling from 'my end' and I had to concede that, for a Bulgarian, he bowled quite well, with just the faintest hint of away swing. Some of his deliveries, bowled at a pace that fluctuated between slow and extremely slow, reared up beneath Hugh's chin but, as expected, he, true to form, one of the old school, eschewed the use of a helmet.

Unfortunately, he soon perished, smiling bravely as he top-edged a ball of Emil's that was chinward bound straight into the hands of a fielder.

"Well bowled, Skip," said I, without really meaning it but, even as I was rewarded with a sincere "Zank you", there was a shout from the perimeter of the field. A commotion! Pete, who was umpiring from the other end, reacted quickest, as befitted a Sidhurst captain, by racing off to deal with whatever emergency had arisen. It was a member of the school caretaking staff, bent on locking the gates and, by definition, locking in our cars. During the ten-minute hiatus I took the opportunity to chat to many of the Wanderers. They seemed a nice bunch of cricket lovers but there was a notable exception that I had noticed bickering from the outset. He not only loudly disagreed with his own position on the field of play, moving backward and forward as the mood took him, but he also had strong views about the competence of his captain. I marveled at the skipper's patience; obviously, chess had something to do with it.

That miserable player approached me and complained that his team would be "batting in the dark" and "Can't you hurry things up?" I thought he imagined I was there in a purely umpirical role and so, humouring him, I reminded him that we, Sidhurst CC, unavoidably delayed, were also not responsible for the car parking problem. For good measure, I felt it appropriate to mention that in any case, it was midsummer and surely it would be impossible for it to get any darker than it was at that moment? Miraculously, no rain was falling.

Pete returned breathless with good news. The caretaker had not only been sympathetic to our plight but had handed over a padlock and key for our exclusive use! That triumph of common sense over bureaucracy, together with our captain's earlier diplomatic handling of the traffic warden situation, impressed us all.

Batting on, a couple of wickets fell but Mat Edwards remained, hitting boundaries with a nonchalant ease that belied the conditions. Everyone heard the tractor before it actually hove into view. Without warning, uninvited, it and its driver hurtled across the park towards us. For one awful moment we feared the pitch would be encroached upon, although it could hardly have been made much worse than it was already. Mercifully, the driver was a man on a mission because, at the last moment, he skillfully veered off, pulled up close to our post and dismounted, cowboy fashion.

We had not been forgotten. He produced a length of rope and, after tying one end to the pole and the other to the business end of his vehicle, he leapt back on, his "I'll have this out in a jiffy, boys!" reassuring those of us who felt that the match had been cursed. The man who I had already decided could moan for England put in his 'four pen'orth' but I pointed out that, in fairness, the tractor driver must have been summoned by someone with initiative. For all we knew he had abandoned his farm or similar to rush to our aid; surely, we should allow him to remove the obstacle?

He couldn't. The rope kept slipping off. We bade him farewell and, as he disappeared into the distance, a few of us amused ourselves briefly by assuming that he would be seeking financial reward at time and a half. The two captains agreed, after further consultation, to reduce the overs to thirty per side; an advantage to our hosts because we had already batted for seven of them, but nobody worried about it.

The Wanderers bowlers bowled tidily and we lost wickets at regular intervals, but Mat held out and became increasingly aggressive as the innings progressed. Why he had to mention that he normally played first team cricket for the club to, of all people, 'Moan for England' was a mystery.

"I'd better get out now, Mr. Ormerod," he whispered, respectfully.

"Why?" I wanted to know.

He told me: "I've sensed a mood swing on the field."

"You had better not!" was my response. "I've not come all this way to lose!"

Only Paul Jackson, aside from Mat, was offering much resistance. Officially, the game was a lowly third team friendly fixture comprised of Mat, a smattering of third and fourth team players and me.

Captain Ivan who, up until that point, had sportingly taken into account the dreadful pitch, now felt compelled to bring on his opening fast bowler, a Sri Lankan gentleman with a sunny disposition who promptly struck Mat on his (helmeted) head with a good length ball that made its way to the boundary as 'leg byes'. Of course, there are no 'head byes' listed in a game of cricket.

Pete was dismissed but he had the presence of mind to request that I leave the field of play immediately to get changed. We were getting desperate. Unsurprisingly, I was due to bat at basement level. Hurrying from the field, hoping that I might not be needed but fearing the worst, I was intercepted by one of the opposition's boundary fielders. He was polite and well spoken. "Excuse me," he said, "are you going to the changing room?"

"Well, yes, I'm actually playing. Why?"

"You can't get in."

"Why?"

"It's locked."

"Have you got the key?"

"No."

"Has anyone else here?" My eyes swept everywhere as I began to fidget.

"No."

"Who has?"

"The park keeper."

"Where is he?"

"He's gone fishing."

I tried my best to look and sound mortified when I reported back to my captain, but fortunately he had seen me batting before and we both knew that any contribution I was likely to make would be coincidental. In any case, on that particular pitch – frankly, on most pitches at that point in my career - getting close to 'in line' would be a 'no no' as far as I was concerned.

Returning instead to umpiring duty, I was in time to witness Mat reaching a well-deserved fifty, whereupon he was particularly severe on the bowling of the Sri Lankan. None of that sat well with 'Moan for England', whose anguished oaths as the ball continued to elude him and his colleagues cheered me immensely. Our innings closed on a total of 137 for 7. M. Harris had made a splendid 72 not out and Paul Jackson had weighed in with a helpful 29 runs.

Luckily, the park keeper had forsaken his extracurricular activity and reappeared just in time to allow access into the tiny pavilion for the between innings tea break. Trooping off the field with our not-out heroes and some friendly fielders, I took the opportunity to interrogate one of the latter, soto voce, as to whether or not the complaining one was like that every week.

"Oh yes," he said, grinning. "His name's James but we call him Benny - but not to his face."

"Benny - the chap in that TV soap?" I had never watched it, but knew of it.

"That's right: *Crossroads!*"

Tea was a spartan affair, completely lacking in, with my usual disregard for political correctness, what I liked to call 'the feminine touch'. Sandwiches of dubious content in all shapes and sizes were pulled from tins, plastic containers and assorted wrappings, leading me to believe that the opposition consisted of confirmed bachelors, or maybe divorcees.

They had done their best, but a familiar voice rang out above the hubbub from the corner of an overcrowded dressing room. "I suppose all the sandwiches have gone?" Naturally, it was 'Benny' moaning again. He supposed correctly. There had not been many to start with although, personally, I had lost my appetite and simply contented myself by nibbling on a couple of salvaged, recognisable chicken pieces whilst stifling a laugh.

There was another minor delay before Sidhurst CC, reinforced by myself, changed, and raring to go, could take to the field when a passing drunk staggered into the pavilion seeking permission to use the grubby toilet facility but, since everything - toilet, changing area and tea room - was all crammed together under the same roof there was understandable opposition from both teams. Conscious of the time, we left the decision to the park keeper who himself seemed impatient to lock up in order to cast his bread upon the water again.

Our skipper, a useful opening bowler, was nursing a shoulder injury and so, reluctant to bowl himself, Pete invited Bob Parsons and Matt Carson to open our bowling when the match restarted. Bob in particular soon had the Wanderers on the back foot and after ten overs their score had limped to eighteen runs for three wickets, all three taken by Bob in five overs at a personal cost of only two runs. At that point - tactically far too early, I felt - Pete tentatively enquired as to the possibility of my 'turning my arm over'. After I had pointed out that I was not really match hardened - not the same, of course, as match fit - having been unavailable, without a game or simply overlooked for many weeks, I failed in my attempts to persuade him to bowl himself or at least look elsewhere. There was talk of 'giving me a game'. My worst fears were soon realised; of line and length there was none.

"Where's the magic, Tone?" yelled Paul Jackson, our wicket keeper, as he threw himself athletically sideways to intercept one of my wilder balls. I stopped myself from shouting back; "Vanished." Damage limitation was the thought uppermost in my mind at the conclusion of an eventful over but, when I demanded to be taken off to avoid further humiliation, Pete courageously insisted that I should continue, presumably on the grounds that, like shares, my form could go up as well as down.

He was very nearly right because something almost magical happened in my next and, as it turned out, last over. A thin edge off the bat of Benny seemed to pass clean through keeper Paul's body! That batsman ran a quick two runs and then glared at me angrily and spat out: "Why do you bowl all the good balls at me and all the shit balls at him?" He waved his bat in the direction of his partner, the genial Sri Lankan who, in spite of a leg injury incurred as he stretched too far to reach one of my looser deliveries, was batting on.

I took it as a compliment. "My bowling is colour blind," I replied, a sufficiently deep riposte that puzzled Benny. In spite of said injury, the happy batsman was busily engaged in dealing with what had become known as 'buffet bowling'. In other words, he was helping himself to mine.

"I'm no good standing up to the wicket," confided Paul; more of a statement than an apology when we briefly chatted at the end of the over. I was in total agreement with him as I consoled myself with the thought that, thanks to my efforts, we now had a game on our hands. My two overs, costing twenty runs, had evened up the contest and there was now something akin to tension in the air.

Benny thick-edged his way to sixteen runs, mostly, luckily, over the heads of, or just outside the reach of fielders before he fell to the bowling of Mark Scott. Our gallant Sri Lankan, hampered by his injury, failed to reach his ground in attempting a risky run and was run out by a superb direct hit on the stumps by young Tim Roberts. He had made 48 runs, many off my bowling but somehow, such was his enjoyment of the game (and my bowling) that I could not begrudge him his success.

The score had stood at 120 for 5 prior to the run-out and with 7 overs remaining and only 18 runs required it looked obvious that a Wanderers victory was imminent. However, Tim bowled, taking a wicket and Pete made a lot of ground on the boundary to take an excellent catch.

The ever-competitive Paul handed over his wicket-keeping gloves to Mat Jones and then, ball in hand, he launched himself at the batsman. Not a sight for the faint-hearted. By common consent, Paul had a reputation for landing deliveries way short of a good length and Benny, looking like he had lost a pound and found sixpence, was now umpiring. On that pitch, in that light, with Matt taking the ball well over head height, a couple of wides were called by Benny. Although I hated to admit it, Benny had a point, but when a ball struck a batsman's leg and was adjudged a wide it was inevitable that there would be a spot of bother!

Paul begged to differ and when harsh words were exchanged between bowler and umpire - the word 'cheat' was used - for a minute or two I thought the game would descend into the farce of fisticuffs. Instead, at the completion of the over, Benny walked away, loudly proclaiming that he had "umpired before Paul had been born". If he had, he must have been wearing short trousers.

Finally, Pete, despite his dodgy shoulder, brought himself on to bowl the final over at, coincidently, his opposite number, Ivan. The Wanderers required six runs to secure the victory, but our captain bowled six balls of such impeccable length and direction that Ivan, flailing away hopelessly without making contact with any of them, made one think that chess was more his cup of tea.

It was all over. We had won by the skin of our teeth. Most agreed that, in spite of the atrocious pitch, the gloomy weather and the delays before and during the match, our perseverance in playing at all was rewarded with a result. The park keeper, anxious to lock up in order to return to his piscatorial activities, hurried us along with indecent haste but, in any case, the primitive bathing facilities had already dissuaded us from lingering.

Two attractive barmaids and real ale were the main features in the local pub but, happily married and of course driving, I merely smiled at the former and drank a solitary pint of the latter. Ivan sat on his own at the bar, smoking his pipe, quietly reflecting on the day's events. Somehow, drawn to him, those of us who stayed on engaged him in conversation. His was a fascinating history. He and some other friendly Wanderers saw us off, and I found myself shaking the hand of Benny and murmuring, "Well played." Hypocrisy. Thy name was Ormerod!

Navigationally unchallenged and unhindered by a peaceful M25, we were back inside Sidhurst Sports Club at 10 pm. It had been a long, eventful day. There had been something about it that reminded me strongly of those vanished, precious halcyon pre-league times. A victory for course cricket and coarse fishing over coarse language, I will always remember it as the day of the irresistible Bulgarian and the immoveable pole.

ANOTHER CAT SONG
(ABOUT MR. TIBBLES)
By Richie Stress

Mr. Tibbles wakes up
And he looks all around,
Arches his back,
And presses his paws into the ground.

It's such a nice day,
See how the sun is high.
Tibbles displays
His feline acrobatic side.

The fascinating Mr. Tibbles,
The acrobatic Mr. Tibbles,
The fascinating Mr. Tibbles.

But you must not stroke him.

I'm just a poor boy,
And I've been locked out of my house.
So I sit on my scooter
And wait for Mr. Tibbles.

Mr. Tibbles comes round to play;
He never quibbles,
He never complains,
Unless you try to stroke him.

Mr. Tibbles – Mr. Tibbles sits and waits,
Yes, yes, yes, yes, yes, Mr. Tibbles fascinates.
He smells the food inside,
And so, he sits and waits.

Has a nibble, then he runs under the gate.
Mr. Tibbles – Mr. Tibbles fascinates,
Don't try to stroke him – Mr. Tibbles fascinates,
Mr. Tibbles – Mr. Tibbles fascinates.

INFINITE FRIENDSHIP
By Houria Gheran

Elena sat in her room before the mirror, practising her lines for the end of year play; she is performing this in a month's time in front of her whole college. She was looking forward to it; she has what she calls the *negative role*, a character named Victoria.

She cannot wait to graduate together with Angel, best friend and class mate, who also plays opposite Elena in the play. Enemies during the performance, they are actually the best of friends. It was five years since Elena and Angel had met each other, Angel having transferred from the Pyramide College to the IVO College in the Netherlands.

Inseparable since they met during that first year in college, they had shared countless memories, weathered storms, and celebrated triumphs together. Now, as they approached their final month, they were determined to leave a lasting impression by performing in the production of *Mean Girls*. Elena was playing a Spanish senorita named Victoria and Angel a character by the name of Regina.

It was Monday, and in the college auditorium the air was thick with excitement. In their usual practice spot, the two girls were going over their lines with enthusiasm and dedication. The stage was set, the lights dimmed – just enough to create an atmosphere of focus and creativity.

"Okay, from the top," Elena said, her voice echoing slightly even though the hall was not empty. She wore a determined expression, masking the nervous energy that bubbled beneath the surface.

Angel nodded, flipping through her script. "Let's nail this scene," she replied with a grin, her confidence bolstering Elena's spirits.

As they practised, their chemistry on stage was undeniable even in rehearsal. They effortlessly fell into their roles, the years of friendship shining through in their performance. But as they ran through their lines, Elena couldn't shake a growing unease. A secret she had buried within for years was fighting its way to the surface, threatening to disrupt the careful balance she had maintained.

Angel noticed Elena's distraction and paused, lowering her script. "Hey, you okay?" she asked, concern etching lines on her forehead.

Elena forced a smile. "Yeah, just thinking about how far we've come," she said, but the weight of a hidden truth made her words sound hollow to her. Angel's eyes softened.

"I know, it's hard to believe this is our last month. But we've got this. We've always had each other's backs."

Elena nodded, but inside, she was struggling. She feared, because of past events, that her secret would be revealed, and she felt it would change everything between them. She took a deep breath, trying to focus on the present moment, on the play, and on the friend who had stood by her side through thick and thin. For now, she pushed her fears aside, determined to make their last performance together unforgettable.

This is Elena's secret: she has been struggling with a severe personality disorder for years. Her true self is honest and kind, but she has an alternate persona, one that is heinous, menacing…and murderous. She has killed before – yet this was unknown even to herself; a classmate of Elena's had been discovered lifeless and bloodied. Did Elena have suspicions about her alter ego's actions? If she did, she buried them deep within. Such actions are not ones to contemplate as being a part of you.

What Elena did know was that her other self tended to emerge at times of stress, at the worst of times, causing havoc in Elena's life and damaging her relationships with friends and family. Two factors concern her now. Firstly, she was aware of that creeping uneasy feeling as Christmas approached, a time that is stressful for many, including herself. The second is that, with horrifying prescience, the character in the play to come is also called Victoria.

Elena has 'come to' in hospital on several occasions with no remembrance of anything that has gone before. Disoriented, her parents have found her with her brown hair in a ponytail and a vivid crimson shade of lipstick on her lips. They are aware that Elena does not like the colour red. Furthermore, on occasion she has spoken Spanish, a language she has never learned. When she awakes, she remembers nothing; her parents are unable to fill in the gaps. Worried and mystified, they are looking for answers from the medical profession.

*

Angel sat in her room at home, oblivious to the fact that her whole world will change in the next few minutes. In fact, the news she is about to hear will have tragic consequences.

Whilst reciting her lines for the play, her father came into the room. He sat down and spoke quietly. "Angel, I have news for you. It will be hard to digest at such short notice, I know, but you need to start thinking about packing your bags. We are moving to London!" He said this with jubilation but some sadness, as he knew Angel would not only be shocked but disappointed.

"What! Why?"

These were naturally the first questions that Angel hurled at her dad. He was patient and explained about the new job commitments that made it necessary, and also the haste at which they needed to move.

"But Dad, we can't move to London. I graduate from college in a month, and I have my end of year play in a week. Let me finish those at least! Then, if we must, we can move."

Her dad, sympathetic, said that he would do his best. After he had left, Angel sat and pondered the fact that she would be leaving her friends, uprooting, and moving from the Netherlands to London. What could she tell Elena? What if she could not complete her last month in college? Strangely, she almost worried more about the play. She was unsure how Elena would react…much as they were best friends, there was something about her actions sometimes…

Next morning, Elena and Angel were in biology class. The bell sounded, signalling the end of the lesson and time to disperse for lunch and rehearsal. Angel asked Elena to stay behind for a few minutes. Perhaps it was not the right time for Angel to talk to her, but her thinking was to tell her now and allow her to have time to process the news. Her motto in life was 'rip off the plaster', because it is quicker and less painful. Most times, this was true. It was not helping holding the news in and only fair to Elena, who had been her best friend for so long; she deserved to know as soon as possible.

Elena smiled. "Come, we are late for rehearsal. I am so excited; I can't believe it is nearly here. After that…who knows? So many things to plan and look forward to together." Elena did not notice that Angel was looking pensive and, at the same time, very nervous.

Angel wondered how to begin the conversation, aware that a few sentences would change the course of their lives and perhaps their friendship. Like Angel, Elena doesn't like sudden changes.

"What's wrong, Angel? You look worried."

"Elena…" She paused.

"Angel, you can tell me anything. We are best friends – just come out with it."

Angel took a deep breath. "I am leaving for London straight after the day of the *Mean Girls* play. Dad, and his new job…" She faltered.

When Elena heard those words, all she could think was that Angel could never be allowed to leave her side, ever.

*

The auditorium buzzed with the electric anticipation of opening night. The lights dimmed, casting a blanket of darkness over the eager audience. Behind the curtain, Angel stood, her heart pounding with a mixture of excitement and dread. It was her final performance together with Elena before she left for London, a future teeming with promise yet shadowed by the sorrow of leaving Elena behind. Elena – her best friend, her confidante – was playing Victoria, the lead. She'd always possessed an uncanny talent for slipping into other personas, but lately, her portrayal of Victoria had taken on a life of its own. Sometimes, it felt like Victoria wasn't just a character but a part of Elena, a darker half surfacing in the moments they were alone.

The play began, and the lines wove together seamlessly, lines that showed many shades of emotion and drama. Elena/Victoria's eyes, when they met Angel's, held an intensity that seemed to burn straight through to her soul.

The scene where Victoria confronted Angel's character of Regina approached, a moment of climactic tension. Victoria's lines were delivered with chilling precision.

"Do you think you can leave me? Do you think you can just walk away?" she hissed. Her grip on Angel's arm tightened. There was no longer any separation between Elena and Victoria; they had become one.

The audience, lost in the performance, had no idea of the perilous reality unfolding before them. The prop knife in Victoria's hand glinted under the stage lights, but in her eyes, Angel saw something else – something real and dangerous. A silent plea escaped her lips, but it was too late. The blade, no longer a prop, was driven into her side, a sharp pain radiating through her body. Satisfactory gasps echoed from the audience, who thought this was a worthy performance, a great part of the act. But as Angel fell her vision blurred, the sounds of the audience in the college auditorium fading into a distant hum.

Angel looked into Victoria's face, which was now a twisted blend of horror and satisfaction. She leaned close, whispering, "Now you'll never leave me."

Darkness enveloped Angel, pulling her into its depths with the hiss of a final breath. And with that breath, unseen, a soul escaped too.

Victoria stumbled off stage, her eyes wild and unfocused. She barely registered the applause, the accolades for a performance that had transcended fiction.

In the silence of the dressing room, Victoria confronted her reflection, her breath coming in ragged gasps. Elena? Are you there?" she whispered to the mirror. But it was not just Elena/Victoria staring back. There, beside her reflection, stood Angel, a ghostly apparition. Her eyes bore into hers, a silent testament to what had transpired. The reflection offered no solace, only a haunting reminder of her actions.

"Victoria did this," Elena muttered, clutching her head as if to ward off the emerging truth. "Victoria, not me."

The room grew cold, the air thick with an oppressive silence. Angel's ghostly form moved closer, and Elena – now fully Victoria – saw the eternal bond she had forged. In her madness, she had ensured Angel would never leave, her spirit forever entwined with Victoria's. Victoria had won. She had Angel forever. And Elena, staring into the glass, could never escape the reflection of Victoria, her darkest self, the one that had sealed their fates with a single, deadly act.

HIS SWEET TREATS
By Jan Brown

He held them close, the keys to his other life. Safely stored in a smart black leather wallet, he kept them with him at all times – heaven forbid if anyone else should find them; they provided entry to his personal pleasure dome. After making his third million in the City, he relocated to the coast. Hastings fascinated him, offering the comfort of familiar seedy backstreets or occasionally the lively pier, with its Kiss Me Quick frivolity. In the summer, he always enjoyed a stroll along the clifftops after his visit was over. In winter, he scheduled his visits to the properties earlier in the day as he disliked the dark evenings. He visited one flat a day as he liked order in his life, but he also loved the thrill of what would be on offer. He licked his overly wet lips in anticipation.

The smallest key opened the door to the top floor flat where he had installed one of his favourites, Ella, a pretty, blonde, middle-aged lady who made outstanding Victoria sponges. He pictured the thick succulent oozing cream, speckled with tiny golden crumbs, and the raspberry jam with no pips. He hated pips; they would stick in the gaps between his teeth. He had excellent teeth, very white, but as his private dentist had informed him at the six-monthly inspection: "Your incisors are very gappy, Mr. Finnigan. A breeding ground for fetid decay." Following that distressing episode he had sought out a less opinionated custodian of the enamel.

Another problem was that he'd eaten so many of Ella's sponges in a very short period (he'd visited excessively) that he'd put on rather too much weight and had to have all his trousers let out. He avoided his GP, fearful of disapproval and the forced regimen of the weight loss programme, but he did stop visiting Ella for quite a while after that. Eventually, the sheer buoyancy of Ella's sponge lured him back.

Finally, surprisingly, Ella had to be let go. Her sponges had stopped exciting him. They no longer rose majestically out of the six-inch springform cake tin that she favoured but stuck stubbornly to the bottom. With persistence, they would flop out, limp and hopeless.

She was last seen serving behind the counter of Costa in St. Leonards on Sea.

He placed a discreet advertisement in the *Guardian* and waited, confident in his belief that they would come.

"I can offer you flat 2B rent free, though obviously you will have to pay your other bills," he told the dark, matronly-looking lady who stood before him.

"What's the catch? I'm not a prostitute, you know."

He recoiled. "Marilyn, this is a reputable building. I don't allow anything like that. But I do have a specific favour I ask of all my tenants. I need you to cook for me one day a week, every week. I need luscious, sweet puddings and cakes to delight the eye and tease the tongue."

Thomas bit into the jam roly-poly, which was Marilyn's offering of the week. He had quickly come to consider her contributions to be somewhat hit and miss. In the previous week she had produced a pavlova that could only be described as spectacular. A melt in the mouth confectionary delight of meringue, whipped cream and marshmallow had made him arch in ecstasy. A week later and he spooned the custard-covered suet into his mouth and chewed doggedly.

"Not bad, Marilyn, but not a patch on last week's pavlova. It doesn't excite me. You need to give me pleasure, not tedium, decadence, not dreariness."

He rolled awkwardly towards the hallway, tugging at his belt. "And I have noticed you keep sneaking weird things into your cakes: nuts, raisins, even carrots. I don't like it. You're just ruining my sweet treats."

Dissatisfied with Marilyn, he became fixated with Candy at 3C. Even her name offered delights to come. Her blonde flyaway hair was reminiscent of spun toffee waiting to be licked.

"Oh sweetie," she would coo, "I have the ultimate fine dining dessert for you. An intense chocolate cake experience. It's to die for."

Thomas spooned the dream mixture into his mouth eagerly, the rush of endorphins surging through him as he reached new heights of pleasure. "Amazing, Candy, one of your best." He ignored the tiny indigestion burn.

"Now try one of these." She advanced on him with a tray of chocolate éclairs. She had already learned he never could refuse a chocolate éclair.

"These are my new favourites." He enthusiastically devoured an éclair, first licking out the cream like a small child. "I must go, Candy, but I will take some éclairs with me to enjoy later."

"Oh sweetie, you are a pleasure to treat. Come back to me soon."

Driving home, Thomas shifted uncomfortably in his seat, the belt seeming to constrict his breathing. "Surely I have some indigestion tablets somewhere," he muttered, pulling into a deserted layby.

He reached for the box of éclairs on the passenger seat. "Can't resist just one more, then look for the tablets."

Out of its box the éclair looked rather sweaty and lifeless, but he took a first bite and then another, then gasped at the waves of pain searing down his arm and crushing his chest.

He screamed, crumbs and cream spluttering from his mouth, all thoughts of pleasurable sweet treats perished in a lonely instant.

DRESSING UP CAN BE DANGEROUS
By Richard Miller

Sam moved to the town a few months ago and, since that time, had got to know a few of the locals and discovered that many were interested in its history. This history dated back to the middle of the 17th century when the first settlers had arrived from England. Those settlers were eventually joined by others from what was once known as the British Isles, as well as from farther afield in Europe. The citizens of the town could rightly claim descent from many countries.

Sam was also interested in history and had a lot of connections in the history 'trade'. This gave him the idea of setting up a shop and museum with artefacts, books, and period clothing. Some items were very old and would only be on display as museum pieces, while others, which were more modern, would be for sale or hire. He hoped his new friends would be able to re-enact days gone by and experience what their ancestors had gone through.

All the residents showed an interest in the new shop and were eager to see it open. Many offered artefacts from their personal collections. One exception was the mayor, David Walker, who was sceptical about where the memorabilia for the shop was coming from. He feared the reputation of the town would be tarnished, especially if outsiders visited and discovered that the items in the shop came from illegal sources.

On one occasion, Sam was closing his shop as the mayor was walking along the road. "I'm glad I've bumped into you, Sam," he said. "I know I've asked before, but I just want to know where you get all the stuff from. Is that too much to ask? I'm the mayor, and I'm just concerned that the reputation of the town will be sullied if things have been acquired illegally."

"That's a strong accusation, Mr. Mayor," Sam said. "Are you saying I've stolen them? Have you any proof to back up your allegations? I took out the lease of this shop in good faith, and the rental and use were approved by the town council, of which you are the head."

"I've read a lot about artefacts going missing from museums and collections around the world. I'm not saying you stole them, but someone else could have and passed them on to you illegally."

"You want proof? Very well. Follow me." Sam opened his shop and led the mayor to his office. Once there, he opened the safe. "Here's the paperwork for the transactions. Take a look."

The mayor scanned a few of the documents and noticed the names of leading museums and private collectors. There was paperwork that showed that more modern items had been purchased from sellers specialising in reproductions of period clothing and other items.

"Looks all above board," the mayor said, sounding sceptical.

"You don't sound convinced."

"I'm not."

"Are you saying these are forgeries? Well?"

There was silence from the mayor.

"Get out of my shop. I've half a mind to consult my lawyers, and I will do so if you make any more accusations against me."

The mayor left, still unsure about what he had seen or heard, but he had no proof.

The day of the grand opening arrived, and because of his position, the mayor was given the honour of officially declaring the shop open. After the shop was formally opened, Sam said a few words, hoping people would fully immerse themselves in dressing up and re-enacting past times.

The mayor, his wife Sandra, and their three children—Peter, Paul, and Mary—volunteered to dress up in replica costumes from the early days of the town. After choosing appropriate outfits from the clothes racks, they each went into a cubicle to change. They agreed to shout, "Here we come!" when they were all ready, to see how the town would react.

The curtains of the cubicles were drawn back, and the five of them stepped out. However, instead of walking out onto the shop floor, they found themselves on a dirt track. To their surprise, there were people in similar clothing walking around, speaking English, but in a strange dialect, using unfamiliar words. One of the people looked very much like Sam, the shop owner.

The mayor's wife glanced behind her and noticed they had emerged from a barn. She had been impressed with Sam's work and his introduction to the shop, but she could not believe buildings could just disappear. Was she dreaming? Had they been drugged and taken to a place set up as a replica of their town from all those years ago?

Walker approached the person nearest to them. "Excuse me, sir. Can you help us? Can you tell us where we are? One moment we were in a shop, changing into these clothes, and now here we are."

The man gave the mayor a quizzical look and said, "I can just about make out what you've said, but it's not like any English I've heard before. A shop, you say? The only shop round here sells foodstuffs, arms, and tools for building. No one sells clothes; we all make our own. As for this place, it's called Rupert's Town."

The mayor was stunned. He knew the name—it was what his town had been called before the War of Independence. The change had been made following the former name's association with British royalty.

"This may sound like a strange question, but what year is this? For us, it's 2024."

"Beg your pardon? You must be dreaming. It's 1647, and we came here three years ago to escape the fighting back home. Have you been drinking? Maybe some of old Tom's strong ale?"

The mayor looked at his family, aware they were as terrified as he was. "No offence, sir, but could I speak to the leader of your group?"

"Samuel! These people want to speak to you," the man called.

The person who looked like Sam strolled over. "Morning, Mr. Mayor, Mrs. Mayor, and children. How do you like your new home?"

"You! But how? What have you done to us?"

"All in good time, Mr. Mayor. Perhaps if you hadn't been so cynical about my shop, I might not have transported you back in time. Mrs. Mayor, I apologise to you and your children, but I don't take kindly to people criticising me."

"You bastard!" shouted Mayor Walker. "I'll get you for this."

"And what will you do? Remember, I'm in charge here, and only I can get you back to where you belong. Now, David—can I call you David? If you do exactly what I say, you can return to 2024."

"And if I don't?"

"David, do as he says," his wife said, now hysterical. "I don't know what he's done, or why, but I just want to get back home, and so do the kids."

"Your wife is sensible, David. I'd follow her advice if I were you."

The mayor cursed under his breath.

"Now, before I tell you what I want, here's a little more about myself and what's happening back in your town and time. I can be in several places and times in history. I'm

98

here, in your town in 2024, at the Battle of Gettysburg, on the Titanic—the list goes on. I've transported many people back in time. Nearly all have done what was required, but some—usually those running from something—have chosen to stay. And a few didn't do what I asked. Most people don't like me, and I've learned to live with that. I guess I'm just cursed to roam forever, taking revenge on those who wrong me.

"I will give you lots of work today, and you could be working up to fifteen hours a day. Are you used to hard work? As for your wife and children, they will work fewer hours, as they weren't cynical. Does that sound fair, David?"

There was no response from the mayor.

"Well, Mr. Mayor?"

"Okay, yes, but I could kill you."

"That wouldn't be wise. The surname I use—or will use in 2024—is Adams, but here I go by Sam Willoughby."

At the mention of that name, a look of surprise appeared on Sandra's face.

"Ah, I see you recognise it, Sandra. I know you've researched your ancestry and the town's history, and I am your 18-times-great-grandfather. So, David, if you kill me, your wife and children will die too. Do as I ask, and you'll return home. What may feel like days, weeks, or months here will be only seconds in 2024."

"Dad, please do as he says!" the children exclaimed in unison.

"See? Your wife and kids agree with me. It's up to you, David."

"Seems I have no choice," he said.

"Excellent. Now, before you start work, there's time to eat and drink—I'm not all bad. Oh, just one more thing. Every day, we pledge allegiance to the British Crown and all its descendants. How does that sit with your revolutionary principles? Another rule to follow if you want to return to 2024.

"Welcome again to Rupert's Town."

VALUE
By Houria Gheran

What is my value? I ask myself.
I have no clue.

How come the one I see as my hero
Calls me worthless, defining me as 'zero'?

My words and opinions have no impact.
That's why none of my relationships
Are intact.

Be it friends or family,
My words and opinions are not taken seriously.
The impact of their hurtful words
Slice through me, like swords.

It takes a while,
But through all the pain, I smile.

What is my value? I ask myself again.
I have no clue.

SHE'S NOT WELL, DOCTOR
By Jan Brown

The darkness was absolute. I dragged my eyelids up a little to be sure. Yes, absolute, thick darkness so still night time, although I could feel a presence. A sharp prick and I drifted back to sleep.

"She's still in there, we think, but we can't get through to her."

"What do you mean, you think? It's been two days now. When will she wake up?"

A familiar voice. Who was that? Who were they talking about?

"Oh, Kerry love, wake up, it's Mum. Can you hear me?"

Yes, I can, of course I can hear you, but what do you want, coming round in the middle of the night? I've got college in the morning. Or is it morning already? Or perhaps it's another hospital visit, I don't know. And what is that strange irritating beeping noise? How is a girl supposed to sleep?

"Mrs. Cooper, we need to stay positive here. There's no reason for alarm at the moment."

Smooth silky tones, definitely masculine, confidence oozing from his public-school backside, no doubt. I curled my upper lip in disdain. Leave me alone, I don't want a posh boyfriend!

"She just moved! My little girl!"

"I'm not sure, Mrs. Cooper. We have been monitoring her carefully and have seen nothing of note. It's very likely an automatic reaction, a little bottled flatulence perhaps."

Cheek! That's it; I'm not having insults like that. Oy, posh boy!

"She's not well, doctor. Shouldn't you be checking her vital signs or something?"

"Very well, Mrs. Cooper, we will do that again." Posh boy, resigned tones.

Ow! What are you doing to my eye? What's that light? Get away.

"Her pupils are responding to light, so she's alive – but at this stage that's all we can say. She needs to wake up so we can investigate further."

I am awake, you oaf! Look, see, I'm here. I'm very much awake.

"Actually, I am observing an increased heart rate, so there may be something going on in there. I do have another appointment, I'm afraid. I'll instruct my locum to pop in later."

Wanker. Posh boy wanker.

Silence and darkness in my world. No, still thick darkness but not quite silence; I can hear a whimpering snuffle, like a dog sniffing around pork sausages. *God, who'd let a dog in?*

"Kerry love, please wake up. I'm sorry."

Not a dog. Mum. Of course, we don't have a dog anymore. What was he called? Bob.

As a puppy his name had been Lucky, but when he'd had a leg off it seemed inappropriate, whereas Bob sounded right... 'bobbing' about and all that.

Mum said she was sorry. What's she sorry for? She loves me: all the hospital visits, the illnesses, the care and concern for me. And once Dad went, it was just the two of us. I've got a vague idea or a memory that she'd resented him sometimes, because he adored me and had such plans for me. And Bob, what happened to Bob? Mum said he'd been a naughty boy and run away.

Where did Dad go? Had he been naughty too? Mum was very angry when I asked her, just before one of my really bad episodes. Then of course she'd been really sorry.

"I'm guilty, Kerry love," she'd say, "guilty of loving too much."

I can feel a pricking in my arm, a warmness flooding through my veins.

"Mrs. Cooper, I'm Dr Hanas, the locum. What are you doing?"

The familiar swamping suffocation sweeping into my chest.

"Oh doctor, thank goodness you're here! Help her, she's struggling to breathe!"

"Crash team." Dr Hanas spoke sharply into his pager "Room five. Urgently."

I forced my eyes open; I could manage a slit. I gasped and choked, desperately sucking at the air and, with a huge effort, clutched wordlessly at the doctor's sleeve, but failed to make him understand that which I'd only just accepted.

"OK Kerry, we're here, we're trying to help you." His voice kind and concerned.

Mum plunged the needle deep into his neck and it stayed there, suspended, as he slumped inelegantly to the grey lino, a look of astonishment across his young, hopeful features.

She looked down and stroked the fringe away from my sweaty forehead. "My poor girl, I do love you so much."

Then she was off screaming down the corridor. "Help, help my daughter, she's had another attack!"

JUST ANOTHER CRASH DAY
By Richie Stress

So, I took out a day
So that I could be
Until I felt the walls
Close in on me

It was far too much
More than I could stand
And no one there
Who could take me hand

I get out of bed
And I feel dumb
Its two in the afternoon
Before the day's begun

Can't be productive
Motivation's gone
Better write it off
Cos life, it goes on and on

I wish I was a wave in the ocean
Wishing like a king who looked broken
A bag of bones with a notion
Just another crash day

If I could be a wise man to carry the answer
Moving fast like some angel dancer
Wanna be all the things I can see
That's just fine with me.

I looked upon the coming waves
So silent and so deadly
I turned around and walked away
And knew that they would get me

When those rolling waves
Freeze against the skin
In their cunning ways
Let the games begin

The space and time it gripped me
Tore me to my true vocation
Beyond the space, beyond the tides
I fell into creation
In the rain and wind
Where the beasts were slain
When the games begin
In the coming days

Now the judgement ends
Can you feel the pain?
That escapes upon the skin.
Just another crash day

Dawnless foreboding
The constant break of just wanting and waiting
Can you tell I'm feeling well?
Or if my heart is breaking.

WALKING TO WORK
By Julia Gale

Monday morning began as usual. I arose at 6:30, had a shower and got dressed, then had breakfast with Alison and our little boy, George, before setting off to catch the 7:30 bus into town.

I arrived at the bus stop ten minutes early, as I like to be punctual. But today, I couldn't help noticing the alarming absence of fellow commuters. It was eerily deserted. Where was old Mrs Jones, who always catches the bus at this hour to shop for her prized turnips? And where was Mr Spencer-Blythe, the barrister who favours the bus over his fleet of posh cars because it's "good for his character"? It was as if the entire bus stop had decided to take a holiday without telling me.

As the minutes ticked by and the bus remained a no-show, my mild concern evolved into full-blown anxiety. It wasn't unusual for buses to be late – though typically they were only late enough to make you late for your plans, not to start questioning your life choices. After a while, with no bus in sight, I knew I couldn't afford to wait another hour for the next one. My boss, Mr Smith, is as old-fashioned as a pocket watch and doesn't tolerate tardiness, no matter how melodramatic the excuse. I considered going home to call in sick, but Mr Smith also disapproves of last-minute sick calls. I could practically hear him tutting at the very thought.

"You've heard the buses are on strike today, haven't you?" a passing cyclist called out with an annoyingly smug grin. I hadn't known – my news consumption is usually limited to whatever gossip floats through the office. The cyclist removed his helmet and of course it was Bob, my next-door neighbour. Bob, who's usually too busy avoiding pedestrians in his car, was now showing off his bike, clearly relishing the chance to be my messenger of doom.

"I would have offered you a lift, but my car is at the garage. If I had a tandem, I'd have let you ride," Bob said, his grin widening to an almost comical width. "I'll let Mr Smith know you're going to be late, shall I?" He knew full well the repercussions of that.

"No need to tell anyone. I'll find another way," I replied, trying to sound braver than I felt.

"Good luck with that," Bob said, pedalling off with an air of triumph, clearly relishing his role in my misery.

It was ten to eight. It was too late to go home and fetch the car. Alison had it today to take George to nursery and get to work herself. We had an agreement – she gets the car on Mondays and Tuesdays, probably because it's the only way I can keep track of which days I can actually drive. So, I made my way to the train station, only to find I'd missed the train by a few minutes. Classic.

"When's the next train into town?" I asked the man behind the ticket counter, who looked like he'd just woken up on the wrong side of a particularly grouchy bed.

"The next one is in an hour. If you'd looked at the timetable, you'd have known," he replied, as if my lack of foresight was the height of human folly. He then pulled the 'Position Closed' sign over the window with dramatic flair. I wondered if he'd been specially trained in customer displeasure. Mr Smith would never tolerate such rudeness at the bank, though I suspect Mr Smith might also have a special talent for dispensing grumpy service.

It was now quarter past eight, and my anxiety had turned into full-on panic. My only option was to walk. Taxis were nowhere in sight and calling one would be a waste of valuable time – plus, a taxi would be as expensive as a small holiday. We were saving for one, after all. I decided to walk as briskly as my not-so-fit self would allow to Weston, a couple of miles away, and catch a local bus from there.

The weather was surprisingly cooperative for a walk. I reached Weston a few minutes ahead of schedule and was about to pat myself on the back when I spotted a young girl, around eight or nine years old, sitting on the pavement. She looked like she'd had a tumble off her bike. With no one else around, I crossed the road to help her, hoping my hero complex would not be judged too harshly by an absent audience.

"Please, sir, I was on my way to school when a car knocked me off my bike and didn't stop," she said, sniffling and looking like she was auditioning for a role in a tragic soap opera. Her injuries were minor – a few grazes – and her bike was damaged, though it seemed more like it had been through a minor skirmish than a full-on collision. I took out my first-aid kit and began treating her cuts, hoping I didn't look too much like a bewildered amateur.

"I think you should see a doctor. I'll call an ambulance and get some help," I said, doing my best to sound authoritative.

The girl looked like she'd rather face a horde of angry squirrels than see a doctor. "No! No doctors, I just want my mum," she insisted, tearing up again.

"You want me to ring your mum instead? What's your name?" I asked. I was really doing my 'Good Samaritan' bit. I glanced around – perhaps the bus strike had kept everyone home. I checked my watch; it was now past 9:30, and I was already half an hour late. Fantastic.

I got out my mobile and Chloe, as she introduced herself, finally gave me her phone number, or at least *a* phone number. I looked down to dial and – whoosh! A hand snaked out, there was a screech of tyres' and she was off. I stood there like a lemon, hand raised as if in farewell, with a bemused expression and an open mouth.

It was obvious, far too late, that I'd been a mug! I'll give her some credit – she could ride that bike, battered or not. Thinking about it, Chloe's story didn't hold water at all – but I still fell for it. The road was too quiet for a recent accident, and her injuries didn't match a serious collision. She wasn't in uniform, didn't have a school bag, and was oddly reluctant to get medical help. I sat on the pavement, head in hands.

As the street grew busier, a passer-by stopped and asked if I was alright.

"I've just been robbed!" I said, trying to keep my voice steady. The stranger, who introduced himself as Dave, an off-duty policeman, helped me up and offered to buy me a cup of tea at a nearby café. I gratefully accepted – who could turn down a free tea, especially after the morning I'd had?

Dave took my details and promised to file a report when he returned to the station. I thanked him and continued to the nearest bus stop. I had just enough change for the fare, but when I got on the bus, the driver informed me that the fare had increased to sixty pence. Embarrassed, I stepped off the bus, feeling like the human embodiment of a 'We're Closed' sign. The other passengers stared as if I'd just attempted a dance routine on the steps.

Deciding to run the short distance over the bridge to the bank, I made good progress until I tripped on a loose paving slab and fell. A crowd gathered, and someone said they'd called an ambulance. The voice sounded familiar – could it be Dave again, or was I just becoming a magnet for well-meaning strangers?

I lost consciousness and woke up in a hospital bed with my arm in a sling, head bandaged, and chest bound. I had several broken ribs. Alison and George were by my bedside. Alison's face was a mix of concern and anger, like she was trying to decide if she should scold me or give me a medal. "You silly idiot," she said, looking at me with a mixture of exasperation and affection. "Why didn't you come home when you realised the buses weren't running?"

"I almost did, but I remembered you needed the car for work and to take George to nursery," I replied, wincing in pain. I couldn't help but think that this might not be the best time to mention I'd also contemplated riding a bicycle to work.

Alison stared at me in disbelief until George broke the silence. "Daddy is silly nidiot," he said, with a beaming smile. Alison laughed, though I could only manage a weak smile. George's observation was spot-on for a three-year-old and had a certain poetic charm.

Alison relaxed a bit and explained that George had been sick shortly after I left. She had called her office and the nursery, then heard about the bus strike on the radio. She had wanted to search for me but couldn't leave George. She called the bank and everyone we knew, but no one had seen or heard from me.

She was about to call hospitals when Dave contacted her. Dave explained the situation and how he had helped me. Alison thanked him and rushed to the hospital with George, feeling guilty for not finding me sooner.

I reassured her that it wasn't her fault and that I loved her before the morphine took effect and I fell asleep, dreaming of a day when public transport was as reliable as George's ability to point out when Daddy had done something daft.

A few days later, I was allowed to go home. I had two messages on the answering machine: one from Dave, saying Chloe's parents had been arrested and asking me to come to the station to make a statement when I felt better, and the other from Mr Smith, informing me that I would now work at the local branch, much closer to home. I was thankful for that. I also vowed never to be in a hurry to help strangers again – at least not without first checking if they came with a warning label.

TREASURE
By Janet Winson

Like a child, mesmerised by the collapsing worm casts all over the beach, I continued to the edge of the sea to find *something*; small, special treasures: pink shells, razor shells, things to put in a seaside bucket. My feet sank into the sand at every step.

I noticed a young boy ankle-deep in the water, playing with a dog. It ran away towards the beach, vigorously shaking itself dry, and I watched the droplets of seawater shimmer in the sunshine and disappear. The boy turned and followed his dog. I recognised him and my heart contracted and leapt at the same time.

"Joe!"

"Mum, why are you here?"

"I just came for the day, Joe. I can't believe it's you. You are so tall now!"

"I'm sorry, Mum, I'm not allowed to talk to you."

"Just tell me how you are, Joe. I miss you so much. Are you happy living here?"

"I love living here, Mum. I never want to come back."

"Is that your dog, Joe? I would have got you a dog, you know I would."

"You'll get in trouble, Mum. They only left me alone for ten minutes; they're on the pier."

My son took the bucket and together we counted the shells. My feet were sand-caked and he teased me with a piece of wet seaweed aimed at my face; the taste of salt made me splutter. He looked sorry and offered me a rough towel to dry myself.

In my heart, I knew he was totally happy standing there, with the sun on his shoulders and the sea crashing into the breakers.

The moment was lost in time, swept away by an angry shout from the pier – and he was gone.

LONGING
By Houria Gheran

Your intense eyes, like liquid chocolate,
Looking at them increases my heart rate.

Your gorgeous smile, a pure delight to see,
When you look at me.

The touch of your hand turns me into flame,
And drives me insane.

Wishing that you will release me
From this sweet torment, which is also an enjoyment.
Oh, how I wish you were only mine!

But you are forbidden and far,
Forcing me to realise that I must resign.

THE JOURNEY
By Julia Gale

My story starts many years ago, when I was a kitten; I was put in a cardboard box and left to die.

It was just outside the dockyard in a place they called Belfast. That cold morning, hearing my plaintive mewing, a docker on his way to work was curious enough to open the box and found me inside. Kind-hearted as well as inquisitive, he picked me up, wrapped me warmly and comfortingly in his overcoat, then carried me into the dockyard.

"Welcome to your new home, little one," he whispered. His tone was kind but also apologetic. "I can't take you home, you see. There's little room, and the landlady—well, cats are not allowed. But," he said, more confidently, "I'm sure you'll make yourself some friends among the other strays in here. You'll be a good mouser with those claws, to be sure."

He gave me a cuddle, then left me alone. At first, while I was young, he fed me each day, but eventually, I was left to fend for myself. I felt lonely and confused.

I hid myself away. Docks and shipyards are noisy, dangerous places for a cat. But before long, I discovered what my claws were for. Very soon, I was out hunting mice and rats with the many other cats, all of whom had made the dockyard their home. Food was available if you worked for it. We often drank out of water puddles on the ground (it rained quite often in Belfast). We also became friendly with the many humans who worked there and seemed to like and enjoy our company; occasionally, a fisherman or two would give us a fresh fish to eat.

Sometime after I arrived, I gained enough confidence to take a stroll by myself around the yards. The ground was white with something called snow, and the place was far less busy than normal. I came across a building I'd not noticed before; the lights were on, and there was just enough room for me to squeeze my way through the door. There were many people in there; it was noisy, but also warm and filled with a sense of jollity. Later, I discovered that the building is known to you humans as a pub. This particular one was called *The Dockers' Inn*.

I came to realise why these pubs are so popular with you humans; you enjoy the taste of the toxic water they serve. I was given a small bowl containing it once. I recoiled in disgust, and the heavy dockers laughed, not all pleasantly. I never did understand why you like that stuff. Is it because it makes you feel happy and start singing and dancing? It didn't always—I have heard raised voices filled with anger and nastiness.

Still, I became a regular visitor to the pub and, before long, made it my home. It was warm and cosier than the blanket on the floor in the warehouse. The landlady, Beth, kept me well-fed and set aside a place in the corner for me, close to the fireplace, where I could sleep.

It was at *The Dockers' Inn* that I was reacquainted with Jim, a thick-set man with a bushy beard whose clothes were always dirty and smelled strongly of smoke. There was something familiar about him, but I was wary at first. I kept my distance because in my world, smoke signals danger. But slowly, my confidence grew, and after a while I found myself sitting on his lap. He would stroke me gently and tell me stories about his many travels.

He told me he worked as a stoker on the big ships. He said he'd been to a country called North America. It didn't matter to him whether I understood him or not (I did, of course). He also hoped he would soon start working on the new ship, *Titanic*, being built in the shipyard next door. He sounded excited at the prospect. I wasn't so excited; I just curled up on his lap. His voice was comforting, and often I would fall asleep.

One day, Jim came bounding into *The Dockers' Inn* and announced to everyone that he had been given a stoker's job on the new ship. Everybody in the pub appeared happy for him; some even bought him a glass or two of his favourite toxic water (I found out later it was called beer). Of course, none of this was of any significance to me. I just lay curled up in what was now our favourite chair and waited for Jim to join me. After a while, he sat down, stroked me for a while, and then whispered into my ear. "I'm taking you home with me—new rooms, new landlady."

Of course, he was my rescuer. Without him, I would not have survived. After some thought, he decided to give me a name and called me King. I liked the name; it sounded important.

Home for Jim was a single room, albeit large, with a shared bathroom in an overcrowded house just outside the docks. It was dirty, smelly, and loud. Jim was a keen cat lover, and now that he had an amenable landlady, he had already adopted another roommate, whom he proudly introduced to me as Jenny. In fact, she had just given birth to a litter of eight kittens, so I feel fortunate that Jim adopted me as well.

At first, I wasn't too sure about Jenny and her brood. She was very protective of them and wouldn't let me near them. Slowly, we became friends, and she began to trust me. She told me that she, too, had been a stray like me. Once Jim had adopted her, she had travelled with him whenever it was allowed on the ships, occupying herself catching mice with the other ship's cats and watching Jim work. It all sounded very exciting.

The time came for Jim to start work on his new ship, and it was decided that the kittens should be found a new home.

118

We were all very upset to be losing the litter, but somehow, I knew that Jenny and I were soon to have one of our own.

It seemed we were allowed to join Jim on his new venture. We left the rented room and moved onto this gigantic ship. We felt so small, but the cabin in which we and Jim lived, albeit temporarily, was just right, and we soon settled in. We set sail for somewhere called Southampton, the first call planned before heading for America.

All was fine until a couple of days into the journey. Jenny began to get jittery and restless; she had the knack of sensing when something wasn't quite right.

Jenny tried hard to get Jim to understand that the ship was unsafe. But naturally, he just put her restlessness down to being about to give birth, and ignored her. After all, we were cats, weren't we? It should be made clear—we could understand humans, but they could not understand us.

I followed Jim into the boiler room, but he told me to move out as it was not the place for cats. Instead, I sat alone in the corner, watching him work well into the night. I think I even fell asleep for a while; it was warm and cosy in there.

Jenny gave birth to our four kittens the next morning, and the same day, we reached Southampton. Jenny was yet more jittery and told me that she desperately wanted to get off the ship.

Titanic was in dock for six days. During that time, we stayed with Jim in a hostel on Northumberland Street. As the date approached for sailing, Jim worried frantically about what to do with the kittens, and during this time, Jenny's anxiety about the ship increased so much that Jim knew something was ailing her.

It was at this time that Jenny came up with a plan. She was not proud of it; I was not happy either, but somehow, I trusted Jenny that it was essential Jim and we did not return to the ship.

119

The hostel was old, and the stairs to the room were steep. It was a simple matter for Jenny to tangle herself in Jim's legs as he descended on the day of sailing. It was not so easy to make sure he was not seriously hurt, but just enough to ensure he could not return to the ship. He broke his leg—not great—but as it turned out, a blessing for him and us. The 'unsinkable' *Titanic* set sail without us that evening.

It was four days later that we heard she had sunk.

Jim lost friends. It was a blow, a sad bitter blow, so much so that he could not face going back to sea ever again. He found a safe job on land and a small but cosy house to live in. He also found himself a companion, Beryl, who also loved cats and moved in with us, marrying Jim. They had a baby some human months later, and we had another litter.

The years have passed. We are happy. But here is the thing:

Jim looks at Jenny thoughtfully sometimes when she is unaware of it and rubs that broken leg, which has never healed fully.

Jim rescued us—and I think, perhaps, he knows that we rescued him.

AUTUMN POEM
By Janet Winson

As the heart expands and beats,
In grief, it can bleed raw pain.
Though still, a tender warmth remains,
Love red as blood.

Sweep up the leaves and trace
The patterns they made.
Savour the cold earth,
And the last late rose.

Pausing to welcome the smallest flicker
Within, that brings comfort.
Sing out the verse,
And await the chorus.

Soon, days will lengthen
And find rhythm and space again.
My world can still spin, open, and expand,
Around this tender space that was planted.

GUNNYSONG
By Richie Stress

I knew today was a bad idea the moment Dave came strolling out of the brush, waving the damn thing like Billy the freakin' Kid—a .357 revolver. Similar to the sort of thing you might see cowboys drawing from their holsters in a duel in some crummy western featured on the Legend channel.

"Hey guys, check this out," Dave said as he trotted eagerly towards us. This was our place, a corner of the woods where we youngsters would congregate during a school break—usually eight or nine kids. With nothing else to do but drink cheap cider, fornicate, and vape.

"Look what I can do." Dave was twirling the pistol round on one finger. It was then that I noticed the safety was off. I should explain that my Uncle Jerry collected firearms and had taught me the various codes when handling them. I needed to warn him before...

Bang!

Everybody stopped what they were doing as the sound rang out around us. The kickback had been enough to jerk it out of Dave's hand. Nine pairs of eyes followed its trajectory until, finally, it landed on sodden earth.

"Dave, what the hell?" Steve said. The noise had rattled him so much he'd dropped his can of Strongbow.

"Don't touch it, Dave, just leave it!" he shouted angrily.

I scanned the group, still stunned.

"Is everyone okay?" I asked shakily when, suddenly, a figure collapsed to the floor, holding his chest. The bullet had lodged itself inside the ribcage of 'Little' Johnny Malone. He slumped to the ground, desperately trying to stem the flow of blood. Before I knew it, the rest of our party had scattered like a pack of frightened hyenas.

"Hey, wait!" I shouted as Dave dashed past me—sweat visible on his forehead, his face expressionless.

I don't know what it was that stopped me from running away like the others. Maybe some deeper sense of morality? Whatever it was, I was alone with Johnny, his breath now shallow and uneven. He looked as if he was trying to say something but was unable to get the words out. I took my jacket off and placed it over him. It seemed like the right thing to do.

"It's okay, Johnny, everything is gonna be alright," I said, because that is the sort of thing you say in these situations, isn't it?

I checked my watch. It was 6:30 pm and the light was fading fast.

"Help me, Chris, please," Johnny silently mouthed. The pool of blood was getting worse.

I had to act quickly; I needed to raise the alarm, so I began to run towards the exit. Looking back over my shoulder, I could see Johnny's body crumpled on the floor, and instantly I knew he was dead.

I stopped and turned back around. The silence was deafening. What did the scene look like now? Me, a body, and a murder weapon.

CATS UNITE?
By Tony Ormerod

Ginger delicately lifted one of his hind legs and licked vigorously at those parts of his anatomy which his fussy female owner was pleased to call his 'bits and pieces'.

In thoughtful mood as he surveyed his territory from the usual vantage point, perched on top of the garage, he had a perfect view of many of the neighbouring houses and gardens which gave him the edge over rivals and enemies, of which there were many.

These ablutions were interrupted by a large cabbage white butterfly, which teased by diving down then veering off at the last moment, thereby cleverly escaping deadly extended claws.

'Once upon a time,' thought Ginger, 'in my younger days I'd have had him.'

He was not the sort of cat who read the newspapers on a regular basis, but this morning, a few minutes before in fact, after devouring a delicious breakfast of coley, his one good eye had caught sight of the headline on what he assumed was the front page of the Sidhurst Newshopper. Not every moggy's idea of a riveting read, but instinct told him that the paper, which had been carefully laid to catch overspill from his frenzied attack on the bowl, held information of some importance.

'ETHICISTS - A PLEA FOR ANIMAL SELF DETERMINATION' screamed the headline. Reading on, he had noted that some Americans, called ethicists, felt that cats, dogs, goldfish, in fact animals of any kind, were being unfairly treated. It was cruel, they claimed, for humans to keep any pets; which confused Ginger. Happy with the status quo, if he was set free, what would happen when his more than adequate food supply was suddenly halted?

There was no way that he could catch the birds and mice which, once upon a time, he had hunted for fun. After all, he was a fifteen-year-old cat. No chicken.

'Good morning, Ginger.'

It was next door's cat looking up at him from the dividing fence a few feet below. The larger, younger black and white of unknown parentage leapt gracefully and effortlessly onto the garage roof and made himself comfortable.

'Don't mind if I join you, do you?'

'Would it matter if I did, Bassett?'

'Please don't call me Bassett, you know I don't like it. The name's Charlie.'

'Can't help it, chum. Liquorice Allsorts! My favourite treats—and with your colouring, well, can you blame me?'

'One of these days,' thought Charlie, 'I'll teach him to respect me.' However, for now, not totally sure whether he would come out on top in a scrap with a legendary fighter, he limited himself to a couple of swishes of his all-black tail and was relieved when Ginger changed the subject.

'Have you seen the article in the Newshopper about cruelty to animals?'

'Yes, but don't you mean The Guardian?' Charlie knew full well that in spite of Ginger's age, experience, and reputation as a heroic fighter, he had been behind the door when the brains were handed out. Point scoring was easy.

'Err, yes, of course, that's the one. Something about 'Ethicals'?'

'"Ethicists," I think you mean.'

'That's them, "Ethicals". Load of codswallop. I would not be surprised if that new Yank President, what's-his-name, had something to do with it!'

'Trump.'

'I beg your pardon?'

'That's his name—Trump.'

'Well, whatever. Any road up, it's rubbish. I'm perfectly happy with my owner.'

For a few seconds, Charlie was stunned and unusually speechless. With a supreme effort, he rallied.

'Owner, owner?' he screeched as his back arched menacingly. 'What are you, a dog in disguise? We cats are in charge and, if anything, we are the owners. It's about time we asserted ourselves.'

Shocked and surprised, Ginger backed away and bristled.

'Oy, watch it, Bassett! Don't call me a dog if you know what's good for you!'

'Don't call me Bassett, you old prat of a cat.'

'Okay, watch it, Charlie. What's your problem? Are you looking for a fight?'

The two cats moved closer together and then the sound of them warming up for action—a typical, unearthly banshee wailing, horribly threatening—caused a few doors to be thrown open. After taking turns, in the old, traditional, familiar ritual, there was a brief lull before Charlie spat out:

'That's your problem, you live in the past. I was going to suggest some sort of action group, an independence movement perhaps, but it's obvious that you would not be interested.'

'Include me out and kindly vacate this garden. Oh, and by the way, don't let me catch you scratching around our flower beds again. Find somewhere else to leave your deposits or you will have me to deal with!'

Bassett, aka Charlie, turned abruptly and leapt down onto the fence. He had to have the last word.

'Please yourself. This could mean civil war!'

LOVE AT LAST SIGHT
By C.G. Harris

"Arthur, dear fellow, have you ever considered the end of the world?"

Taking the pipe from my lips, I stared at Hargreaves thinking his question rather extraordinary.

"Eh?"

It was Friday, and he was making his customary weekly visit to my rooms; an agreeable social pastime not normally given over to thoughts of Armageddon. There had been little in his manner to indicate remarkable matters on his mind; he was not given to agitation, due no doubt to his scientific training, and in my drawing the curtains, pouring us post-prandial sherries and settling down before the fire, I suppose I had indicated my content to allow the conversation to flow where it would at the end of a busy week.

Sitting for a while in amiable silence, the gas lights low, comfortable in high-backed chairs, I had been smoking a pipe lit by a taper from the fire. Occasionally holding his glass aloft, the slumberous, crackling flames he had been studying were refracted in the crystal; it seemed to give him pause for thought.

Now, I use the word 'refracted' in deference to his area of expertise, which is that of the concise and physical. I may say, more precisely, astronomical, his study being that of heavenly bodies: suns, planets, stars, and such sort – paraphernalia alien to my own sphere, which, being a medical man, is that of the mind and body. I have often considered our friendship abetted by our contrasting interests in the small and the large, the bringing together in converse of the micro and the macro, the mysteries of the human and the extraterrestrial. All of a sudden, he had seemed to collide the two.

"Eh?" I repeated

Smiling, he said: "End of the world. Earth, gone. Humanity gone with it."

"Well. I daresay it has crossed my mind – when the sherry has been poured too liberally."

He laughed, rather ruefully, I thought. "Do consider it further. When the sherry allows of rational thought, of course. However, I will take another glass – I do not wish to think of the matter myself while I am sober. Until I am sure…"

I poured him another measure. "Sure? Of what? What can you mean?"

He arched a brow then stood and walked deliberately to the window. Drawing back one of the drapes, he tilted his head up at a late autumn crystal sky. His face was a study in concentration and he asked me to join him. "What do you see?"

"Oh, on a night such as this about a billion stars, that's all."

He smiled. "Anything else?"

"Well, the moon, of course. Beautiful and not quite full."

"Yes. Beautiful indeed. And above and to its right?"

"A star?"

"Jupiter."

"Ah."

He narrowed his eyes and peered with ferocity. "Beyond Jupiter. Can you see anything?"

I tried. "I see nothing, I'm afraid."

He rubbed his eyes. "No, of course…without implements…ah, well, well. Perhaps I am wrong. It has been known."

"Wrong?"

Suddenly smiling, he turned and clapped me on the back in his old way. "Forgive me, dear friend. To the table. Bring out the knights, the rooks, the queens, the pawns! Let two bachelors of middle years do battle and see if astronomer can yet beat doctor at the beautiful game!" Emptying the box, he muttered: *"And meteors fright the fixed stars of heaven."*

"What's that you say?"

"Nothing. A little Shakespeare."

Hargreaves left as the Westminster Tower struck ten, a Hansom taking him from the door; my thoughts were disturbed ones when I retired. I loved the dear fellow – but the devil take him, for a restless night!

*

The following week saw a return to mundanity, and yet not quite; in my profession encounters with those of unhealthy bodies, disturbed minds and emotions can never truly be dull. Surprising, however, was the receipt of a telegram from Hargreaves on the Wednesday asking me, as a particular favour to him, to call upon an elderly lady; it was not clear how their paths had crossed. It was so unlike him to be concerned with anything less than the celestial that this was a significant change in him, I felt. Had he at last turned his gaze from the heavens to his fellow man? Unlike myself, who in youth had loved, and later lost, Hargreaves, a dark yet greying, good-looking man with moustache, had devoted his life to his work.

Nevertheless, that evening, I found myself outside a terraced house in Battersea, a stone's throw from the murky, lapping waters of the river. I was tired and the location, by no means salubrious, was beyond the sphere of my normal rounds but it had never crossed my mind not to call. I did not know what to expect but when my knock was answered – there was no bell – I was surprised to find a nervous, at first-sight plain woman, above the age of thirty and five, I hazarded. Her face was pale and made more so as framed in tied-back, dark hair, albeit this streaked with early grey.

"Sir?"

"Doctor Lawson." I enlightened her.

I heard a prolonged coughing from within, consumptive it seemed to me, even from here. "May I come in…?"

The woman looked puzzled for a moment. "It is kind of you to call, sir. How did you…?"

"Why, Mr. Hargreaves, of course." I raised my brows in question.

A weakened voice called out: "Mary…the gentleman from the gardens…" followed by a further bout of coughing.

Mary flushed just a little, nodded, and stood aside.

The interior had a hint of faded gentility about it. The living room was small and poorly decorated, but the mantle adorned with silver and brass nick-nacks and the wall with two or three accomplished oil paintings; one was that of a countryside view and another of the very lady that reclined before me on a threadbare patterned sofa, albeit in her earlier and healthier years. I commented on the pictures and the dame, in between coughs, was anxious to inform me that her daughter Mary had painted these.

The young lady in question sat now on a stick-back chair by a window in the corner of the room. Her head was down and she was concentrating fervently on some embroidery; I will say tapestry rather, as she was weaving a pattern into the fabric as she went. Other completed pieces of brightly coloured woven cloth lay on a table and when I glanced at these, I could see that they had been created by a loving, artistic hand.

I turned to the lady on the couch but did not approach too closely when she coughed. It seemed evident to me even now that, though not fully progressed, a disease of the lungs had taken hold.

Questioning her carefully, I was not surprised to learn that these were two ladies of upper background fallen on hard times; a gentleman officer husband (and father) taken from them at Laing's Nek in '82 was one more casualty of that unnecessary Boer War. There was no doubt in my mind that the reduction in circumstances and removal from an estate out of town to this less than satisfactory abode had contributed to the ill health before me. Here is an irony: the best (and only) cure for consumption is fresh air, rest, and the gathering of strength thereby. Ideally a return to the country would be best, and I put this to her.

"Were it possible, Dr. Lawson, I would…perhaps a small, rented cottage, could I but find such a thing. In the meanwhile?" She smiled.

"In the meanwhile, Mrs Brightwell, take the air as best you can; go to the gardens, keep windows ajar – though not too much. And-" I glanced in the young lady's direction "-your daughter must take care she does not succumb. Close proximity is not recomm-"

Mary looked up quickly. "I will care for Mama, Dr. Lawson, whatever happens."

"Yes. Yes, of course." I smiled at her. I rose to take my leave then, as an aside, asked if I could see what she was embroidering.

Hastily, she turned it face down and said, with reddened face: "It…is not yet finished, Doctor."

I nodded and then reassured them I would return in a week.

Thanking me, the young lady saw me to the door. I paused as she closed it upon me; an early moon had allowed me to see in its softening light the face of a woman not so plain after all, radiant with an inner goodness perhaps; destined, however, to be alone whilst remaining so ever

131

loyal to Mama. Yet this loyalty was the provider of her radiance.

I walked home across the river, where Old Father Thames resides beneath its many arches; a romantic yet muck-ridden god, of course. As I walked, I wondered what motif Mary wished to keep hidden to herself.

*

On the Friday, it seemed that Hargreaves knocked with less than his usual gusto and when I opened, he entered and shrugged off his hat and coat in a distracted manner. Before I could remark he had moved swiftly into the drawing room and whilst I hung his garments, I heard the clear sound of decanter against glass; the brandy was out earlier than was our wont. Nevertheless, I decided to join him and when I had filled my own glass, I bid him sit then glanced at him curiously. I waited patiently for him to speak; he threw back the brandy then poured another. Finally, he smiled a wan smile and ran one hand through hair that seemed greyer than a mere week ago.

"I've had a reply from Higgins…"

"Oh? Er, Higgins?"

"Higgins, Higgins," he replied, testily. "Of the Royal Astronomical Society. And a further confirmation from Sir James Aintry."

"Ah, now he I *have* heard of. Former Astronomer Royal? Hargreaves smiled at last. "I'm impressed."

"Confirmation…with regards to?"

His smile faded and he stood downing his brandy as he did so. "Why, the fact that an asteroid of considerable dimensions will collide with our home planet in…" He took out his pocket watch to glance at it then laughed at the absurdity. "Oh, six weeks or so…"

I leaped from my chair; the spilt brandy seemed of little consequence. "Good God!"

"I fear the Almighty is not with us on this one," he said, grimly.

"Are you sure of this? What does it all mean?"

"Please do sit; let us both sit. I will explain. It means," he spoke patiently, "that an asteroid of this size, approximately six miles in width, travelling from the close reaches of the asteroid belt at 70,000 miles in every hour – it will speed up considerably as it nears – will impact us with enough force to-"

"Yes?"

"Destroy us all," he finished.

It is difficult to know what to say or think when the previously inconceivable is laid before you in such stark terms. Of course, I did not believe it – or would not. Hargreaves had regained his composure and was relating it all in such a matter-of-fact way I felt that we were having one of the many cosy philosophical discussions in which we had indulged over brandies in the past. He seemed almost light-hearted. Perhaps when faced with the inevitable, certain of us are capable of such *laissez-faire* – I was not one of them and was sure that, had I looked in a mirror, I would be wild-eyed and ashen faced.

We both lit pipes, which calmed me somewhat.

"And now?" I asked. "Who else is aware of this? Who else *should* be aware of this?"

"Now? Well… Firstly, I am meeting Higgins and Aintry. *Who* to inform? Um, governments, I expect." He gestured vaguely. "Of course, it will be a short matter of time before other astronomers make the same discovery. They may have already done so." He puffed on his pipe and the smoke rose lazily upon the heated air from the fire.

"What can be done?"

"Done?!" he laughed. "Why, nothing, of course! Now, listen…listen, my dear friend. It may be that there is hope. Hope that not *all* of mankind, not *all* of fauna, flora, will be destroyed. In which case, the human race will rise again. Perhaps better, perhaps stronger, perhaps with more compassion than ever before."

"Bit late for us," I said, gloomily.

He laughed again, the familiar laugh I had known since our university days. Then, with seriousness, he proceeded. "This is how I see it panning out, what I fear. First, there will be disbelief by those in authority. Then the facts will be laid before them and they *must* believe. There will be a numbness, followed by the inevitable question of what we can do to stop it; the answer will be nothing. For the altruistic, it will then become what limitations can we place on the damage and loss of life; the answer will be very little. The selfish will consider what they can do to save themselves, their families. The answer may be shelters deep within the earth; only the rich and powerful will have that option and they have little time to prepare and small chance of success. Once the masses find out, both about their imminent destruction and that the wealthy are saving themselves, there will be panic, there will be jealousy, there will be violence, there will be looting.

"For those who have religion and belief, there will be prayers to an unseen god to be saved – to which the response will be: nothing. The world on all continents will become a cesspit in which every person is for themselves or their loved ones. Humankind will descend into oblivion amidst a sea of lawlessness – with small pockets of philosophical acceptance and perhaps some love. That is what I fear," he concluded.

"Good God!" I spilled the brandy again and dropped my pipe.

"There you go again, dear friend, with the god thing." He closed his eyes. "Yes, perhaps some love. *'Speak low, if you speak love'*," he murmured.

I looked at him curiously, then he opened his eyes.

"Shakespeare again. Get the chess out," he said.

*

Mrs Brightwell died two days before my next visit. It was Monday. The sombre premises were made even more so by the drawn curtains and the presence of a small wreath which hung on the door; my heart sank as I knocked. I wondered why Miss Brightwell, Mary, had not called me at signs of deterioration then realised I had not left my calling card upon my first visit. When she opened the door, she was dressed in loose dark clothing that contrasted with the paleness of her face, although the circles under her eyes were almost as dark.

Politely, she ushered me in. The drawing room had a low light but I could see that the great mahogany clock on the wall had been stopped, a customary old-fashioned ritual; the mirror had been turned to face the wall and photographs turned face down. In the corner was –

"Hargreaves! Why, what – how?"

He smiled; it was too dimly lit to see if the smile was sheepish or not. But his voice betrayed an amalgam of wonder and disbelief that he was sitting here himself. "I called yesterday, Lawson, to see if Mrs. Brightwell was improving." His voice dropped. "Too late, I fear. I helped arrange the death certificate. Miss Brightwell…Mary…has no one-" He looked at her as she busied herself with a pot of tea and cups for us. "No one. At times like these, one needs support and," he hesitated "friendship." The teapot rattled loudly.

Mary poured the tea. Although there was sadness, there was a sense of something else in that pouring, in that ritual so beloved by the English, something uplifting.

I smiled inwardly. "I see. Well, I thank you, Hargreaves." I paused. "You have always had the kindest of hearts, my friend." I meant this sincerely. I drank my tea and rose to

135

go. "My sincere condolences, Miss Brightwell." I gave a small bow and, espying the tapestry I had seen before lying face down over a chair, said, "I hope, Miss Brightwell, there will come a day when sadness passes and you will complete your beautiful works." I nodded briefly towards it.

She picked it up and held it towards her so I could not see. But she smiled. "There will, Dr. Lawson." She glanced towards Hargreaves.

Hargreaves roused himself and saw me to the door.

"Well," I said.

"Well," he replied.

"Does Miss Brightwell know the end of the world is nigh?" I said, wryly.

"No," he said, "but I will tell her. And do you know? I think she will take it rather better than you may imagine; she is that kind of woman." He shook my hand, closed the door, and left me to my thoughts as I wandered home. Occasionally, I looked towards the heavens to see if I could spot the architect of the world's destruction.

*

Over the next three weeks Hargreaves visited just as usual, although I had the impression that in between these calls he was not just gazing at the heavenly bodies but at one more important to him that was closer to himself in Battersea.

During these weeks, worldwide, things began to happen as Hargreaves had predicted. We sat and drank and smoked pipes while he described how he and other eminent persons convinced disbelieving governments of how little future they had left. Can one blame them for their incredulity? After all, they were being told that four billion years of earth and two hundred thousand years of humanity would soon be gone. Acceptance of the facts reluctantly followed. The reaction was stark and in accordance with how Hargreaves foresaw it happening.

Occurrences at home and rumours and reports from newspapers around the world convinced me that the foreseen panic, riots, lawlessness, and the 'everyone for themselves' attitude was to the fore. People scurried from place to place like terrified and bemused mice. Those that didn't, hid, sometimes under the covers of their own bedclothes. In places, aspects of civilisation burned, set alight by those with wild-eyed hate borne of panic and terror. It was frightening to read and see but, given that oblivion beckoned, it was natural. Oh humanity, brought down! But then:

Something remarkable happened. We underestimated mankind's innate empathy, goodness, and sanity. For to panic, strike out, burn, loot and pillage is meaningful only if there is an escape; here there was no escape. To what avail are those things? Reflect and look deep into your soul. Focus on the ones you love. Cherish your family if you have one and fill your remaining time with them. If you love food and drink, satiate yourselves. Conversation? Talk of matters great and small with those to whom you have never spoken. With nothing to protect, smile at strangers. Elope – for an eternity. Confess your love, platonic or otherwise, to those whom you should have done long ago, before forever descends.

The chess board sat laid out and placed just so on the coffee table; across from it was an empty seat. My heart shifted within me and I ran from the room.

*

I see it now.

A dot bright in the firmament, shooting across and down the vault of a cobalt sky. Brighter than Venus now. I run for the river and across a bridge that soon will shelter Old Father Thames no more; throwing my hat to him, I bid him farewell as I run. My heart and legs must hold strong.

137

The house is there, sombre no more, curtains wide and windows open. Upon the door there hangs something, I cannot see; not a wreath. Now I see – square, bold, elaborate, in colour red upon white and green, two hearts intertwined; bouquets of flowers run in thread along the side. Mary's tapestry. Her symbol of love that she found at last.

I turn and look towards the river. Families, loved ones and strangers alike, hand in hand looking skyward. But where is… There! There! Hargreaves and Miss Brightwell are kissing and then their hands entwine.

"Hargreaves!... James! James!"

He turns at my cry and, with urgency, waves me to them; he and Mary with smiles hold out their arms to me. Above us, something brighter than the sun, alien and indifferent to our fate, is now upon us; but it is too late to halt our embrace.

ABOUT THE AUTHORS

The TEN GREEN JOTTERS of Sidcup:

Jan Brown

Jan Brown, aka Emily the Writer, has always loved writing, ambitiously penning her own Starsky & Hutch story at the age of 12, although she never actually allowed anyone else to read it.

Jan has had a number of articles, interviews and short stories published and is a prize winner in, and contributor to, The Monthly Seagull magazine and to the Charlton Athletic fanzine. She lives with her husband, Richie Snashall (reader, I married him) and still loves anything furry with four legs.

Glynne Covell

Married, with two children, and grandchildren, her hobbies of travelling, history, and calligraphy all have links with her writing for which she has a very special passion (this, and chocolate!). She is delighted to be able to contribute to this, the fourth anthology by the Ten Green Jotters of Sidcup.

Julia Gale

Originally from Carlisle, then brought up in Southampton, Julia moved to London in 1995 after marrying her husband, Colin. Julia was a prodigious early reader as a child. Always with a book in her hand this may well have fuelled her desire to become an author, and she began by writing poems for the local church magazine. Over the years she has had a variety of jobs but since being married has been a full-time mother and house wife, occasionally finding time to do voluntary work; with Colin, she has three grown up daughters and a disabled son. Her hobbies are cooking and gardening.

Her observations on people, the real-life situations they find themselves in and life's many ups and downs are reflected in her stories.

C.G Harris

C. G Harris hails from Kent, England, UK. He is a former winner of the *William Van Wert Award* for a fiction short story. His book *Light and Dark: 21 Short Stories* was shortlisted for the *"Words for the Wounded" Independent Author Award*. His second collection, *Kisses from the Sun and Other Stories* was released in June 2020. His third book of stories features the 1940s Manhattan private investigator, Aaron Baum, and he is currently writing a second volume of cases.

He has a wife, two daughters, four grandchildren, one dog and a cat. He plays the guitar, ukulele, and juggles...although not necessarily all at the same time.

For more information about the author and his books go to website: www.cgharrisauthor.com

Houria Gheran

Houria was born one of five siblings in war-torn Afghanistan; from there she and her family travelled to the Netherlands where she lived until she was 17 years old, and thence moved to England. Her background and travels, and her love of reading from a young age, inform her writing and have also enabled her to speak five languages (Dari, Dutch, English, Spanish and Turkish).

Her love of literature began at an early age with a visit to the library and an introduction to the magical world of Roald Dahl and The Big Friendly Giant. inspiring in her the desire to create stories that readers want to immerse themselves in whether they be romance, adventure, horror or fantasy; she also has a deep love for writing poetry, her young niece being her first muse in this regard.

It is rare to find Houria without a book or a notepad to hand enabling her to read or write wherever in the world she goes.

Richard Miller

Richard has lived most of his life in Sidcup, birthplace of the Ten Green Jotters. Although much of his working career was spent in London as a Network and Telecommunications Manager in a Government Department, his job also required him to visit more exotic locations including Barbados. India, South Africa, and Thailand.

He is a season ticket holder at Chelsea and enjoys real ale, whisky, blues music and history. At home Richard has several hundred books and records plus several bottles of single malt whisky. He is a member of several historical societies and is on the committee of one of them. Richard is researching his family history and has traced one branch back to the 17th Century.

Tony Ormerod

Derby born, and dreaming of journalism, at 16 Tony inexplicably rejected a job offer with the local *Evening Telegraph*. Employment in the warm bosom of Local Government beckoned and then, migrating way down South [Hove], he progressed to Bromley Council where he was later declared surplus to requirements. A career in financial services led to early retirement and an ambition to do nothing was achieved.

Occasionally, this idleness is interrupted by articles published in the aforementioned newspaper plus a couple more in the 'Best of British' magazine. After 55 years he remains married to the same lovely wife. She pleads anonymity.

Richie Stress
Richie has always liked words. He has used them to write short stories, scripts for television and award-winning poetry. In 2008 he was talked into studying for a Creative Writing degree by a very enthusiastic lady from the Open University…and which he completed a mere seven years later. He lives in Orpington with his wife and his favourite animal is the snow leopard.

Janet Winson
Janet hopes that you enjoy her two stories and poem within this collection; they all have their roots in family life and past events - with some poetic license!

Reading has been a big part of her life from earliest days, plus a love of cinema and theatre that has continued and grown during retirement. The writing bug came later and she was greatly inspired after taking a Creative Writing course during which she met other like-minded individuals and they went on to form the Ten Green Jotters writing group. Meeting monthly, Janet and the rest of the group share literary creation and friendship. She hopes you enjoy this fourth collection of stories from the group.

Lilly the Dog
Lilly is the honorary member and mascot of the group. She is ten years old, a springer spaniel, and her interests consist

of eating, "squirrel-chasing" by day and "fox-watching" in the evening. She was inspired to join the group after reading that Timmy the dog was a founder member of the Famous Five. She has not displayed any literary talent as yet, but the rest of the group remain optimistic

More books by the Ten Green Jotters (available on Amazon):

Literary AllShorts (Vol.1)

AllShorts of Crime

Fractured Times

Visit their website at www.tengreenjotters.com for more information about the group and the books.

Printed in Great Britain
by Amazon